Remo Went Down

Mike McCrary

Dedicated to the good people I know and love,
but not you.
You? You know why, Dickhead.

Part I

Remo's still the goods, baby.

1

Remo Cobb is a fucked up mess of a man.

A worn strap of beef jerky barely able to stand upright. It's a real struggle, given what Remo's been through, but still, there he stands scanning over the tattered remains of his once glorious NYC monument to success. Not long ago, his multi-million dollar condo was the picture of New York elite living.

Now?

Now it's a busted-up shitbox. Simply a pile of broken things that used to be worth some serious scratch. Not much in the way of glory here anymore. Elite living? Not even close. That super expensive, super special glass thing that gay-as-hell decorator picked up for him in SoHo? That one-of-a-kind picture of whateverthefuck? Those things and more are shattered into millions of overpriced pieces, scattered across the floor in a super special spread of useless debris.

At one time, Remo's suit was the proud uniform of a big-time, big-money attorney. Custom tailored, high-end threads worked and crafted with amazing precision by a man named Mario, working out of The Plaza. After Remo's little conflict in the Hamptons, however, this five-figure suit is now a torn and frayed disaster. Covered in sweat, blood and fear, but with just a touch of redemption. It's the suit he wore when they wheeled him into the hospital. Despite all this destruction to everything he owns, there's an odd smile plastered across Remo's face.

Crooked, to be sure, but there is a smile.

A look of relief mixed with joy on his face, his eyes locked in a thousand-yard stare. Despite the demolition of this earthly wealth and the physical pain he's endured, he got what he wanted. What he really wanted. What he set out to get done.

He met his son.

He met Sean.

Remo grows an even bigger smile. A pure smile.

The cost of the goods that have been reduced to rubble before him is staggering, but he simply does not care. He finds an unbroken highball glass up high in the cabinet. It somehow survived Hurricane Mashburn. *Brave little guy,* Remo thinks. *It must have been a rough storm to ride out.* Remo serves himself a long pour of Johnnie Blue then moves on to the living room. Swatting away a coaster, a coffee cup and the scraps of a broken dessert plate, Remo takes a seat in a leather chair. Drinking in slowly and deeply, he lets the scotch go to work.

It burns the good burn.

His brain unwinds.

Thoughts unspool the insanity of the recent events.

Thoughts of his house in the Hamptons and the war fought (and won) against the Mashburn brothers. All the blood spilled. Some of it his. More of it theirs. Guns blasting. Shells bouncing. Bullets pounding. Hollis the hitman coming to his rescue. Lester putting a period on the thing by cutting off Dutch Mashburn's head.

Remo shivers a bit off that little golden memory.

Can still see Lester doing it. The cutting. The hacking. The sounds of it.

He drinks more. Pops a pill. He's sore as shit.

His mind drifts back to Hollis and how pissed off he was at Remo. Even though he came back to help Remo out, Hollis was so damn hostile about doing it Remo's fairly sure he will never see nor hear from the man again. Hollis will bounce the hell off the planet with his wife and kids and never be seen again. They will become ghosts. Hollis knows how to become thin air. It's what he does. Hollis is a professional killer with some special skills, and those special skills are the reason Remo knows the man.

Remo defended Hollis successfully a few times, and helped him take care of some other legal problems before they became fully fucking realized shitstorms. Remo helped with things, like where to find a clean car. Where to find a safe house. Where a few stacks of *fuck you* money were located. Those bits and bobs and more. Remo and Hollis were decent enough friends. Until Remo let his dick wander a bit.

"You fucked my first wife, got a hand job from the second, and tried to work a three-way with the third," is how Hollis recalled it. Remo knows he's not wrong.

Remo takes another slug of Blue.

He considers Hollis a friend, despite the roadblocks.

Hollis is a good one.

"Oh well," says Remo, "fuck it."

Big slug of booze, followed by another long pour, filling his glass.

His brain now slips over to Lester.

Ah, Lester.

The former criminal and current man of the Lord. Not to mention a completely insane killer with a borderline personality disorder. Lester was a member of the Mashburn crew until he went to prison and found God. He was a new man when he came out. Lester left the Mashburns—actually he tried to kill the Mashburns—and then set out on a righteous path. He considered Remo to be a sheep in desperate need of Lester the Shepherd. He truly believed Remo needed his special brand of saving in more ways than one. Remo watched Lester get shot in a Chinese food joint, then watched Lester show up later, a couple of days ago in the Hamptons, to cut off Dutch Mashburn's head.

Remo shivers again.

Drinks more.

Then there's Sean. His son. His boy. The child from his failed marriage. Remo takes some pride in the fact it's his only marriage. He still cares for Anna, but knows she's better off without him. Most people are. She's a good person. Smart. Strong. Good mom. Remo has no illusions of reconciling with her, despite his recent moral turn. Anna has warmed a bit to him recently, but nowhere near thawed enough to even vaguely consider taking him back on a fulltime basis. He knows he fucked all that up years ago, but he's truly grateful to her for letting him meet Sean.

She didn't have to.

He knows it.

Remo had given her plenty of reasons not to.

The look on his son's face when they met in that hospital room for the first time was worth everything he went through with the Mashburns. Remo would do it all again, if he had to. He'd rather not, it was a bitch, to be clear, but he would do it for his boy.

Another drink.

He thinks on the conversations he had after Sean and Anna left the hospital room.

Conversations with cops and lawyers.

Angry cops and lawyers.

Conversations that contained words like *disbarred, criminal charges, seizure of assets* and *you're fucked, you are completely fucked* and *fuck you, Remo.*

Big drink.

Now his brain slides to the future.

Remo's future.

Doesn't look all that rosy.

"Shit."

Gulp.

2

"You're saying I'm not going to practice law?"

"Remo, we talked about this. You're not practicing shit anymore. The pain pills dicking up your hearing?" Victor asks.

Victor is Remo's boss. The biggest, baddest partner at the firm. He's known as a titan in the criminal-defense-attorney circles around the city. He has a soft spot for Remo, but in this case there's only so much he can do for the guy. Remo is toxic with a capital T. Victor has his phone gripped so tight in his fist it's about to snap.

Remo called him from his condo looking for a little help and hope from his boss. Neither help nor hope is going well.

"There has to be something," Remo says.

"Your place in the Hamptons is filled with blood, bullets and bodies. The bodies, the Mashburns, were your former clients. The firm's former clients. One of them sans his head, I might add. There are also rumors floating around that you threw the case against them, which would more than explain why they would come to your house with murder on their minds."

"Dammit, Leslie," Remo mutters.

"What?"

"Nothing."

Leslie was a casual sexual acquaintance, mutually casual, and also a New York Assistant District Attorney. Remo gave her all the evidence he had against the Mashburns and their crew, then he dug up the money they stole and gave it to a good cause. Most of it, at least. Leslie must have blabbed about all that. She was the only one who could connect the dots. Can't blame her. She has to watch out for her own ass too. Still, it pisses Remo off.

Remo pauses. Thinks of speaking, knows he's got nothing. Stops.

Everything Victor is saying is true.

"You've got a meeting. A damn important meeting tomorrow afternoon with your buddy, Detective Harris."

Remo chokes as he gulps some Blue. "Harris? He hates me. He'll eat my heart and toss me in the street."

"Yes. Yes he will. Look, I can't help you. I want to, but I've got to create some distance. You're a toxic prick at the moment." Victor takes a breath, looks at a picture of him and Remo skiing in Vail. "You know the drill. Keep your mouth shut with Harris. Let the cops talk and work the best deal you can." Victor dumps the picture in the trash.

"What about money?" Remo asks.

"What money?"

"My money."

"Your assets are frozen until the Feds can sort all this out."

"No severance package from sweet, sweet Victor?"

"I can't. Wouldn't look great. Maybe when this is all over. If you need some cash to get you through, I'll be glad to—"

Remo hangs up.

He begins to work the floor at a feverish pace. Moving back and forth, back and forth, letting his mind run ripshit. Racing to his closet, he sees most of his suits are gone—no idea where they went—but there are still a few pairs of overpriced jeans and some shirts he can live with for a while. Moving to the bedroom, he dumps the things from the closet onto the bed and then fishes out a few pairs of underwear, some socks and a couple of T-shirts.

His phone rings.

It's Alex Trip. A law school friend Remo hasn't spoken to in a few years. Not since that little incident in Vegas. Long story. Odd and ugly. Shit happens. Remo tries hard to remember if he owes Alex anything or what pile of shit he might be stepping into if he answers the call. Remo quickly decides the risk is worth the potential reward and that he can use all the friends he can get right now.

"Alex?"

"Remo, long time. Look, I hate to dump this on you. Heard about your troubles. Not sure if you're in a cash crunch or not but I got something with my brother, Jasper. Might help you out. Nothing crazy, just a little money for a lead of sorts."

"I'm in."

"You want to hear what he wants?"

Remo sighs. "Fine."

"He wants to be put in touch with some bank robbers."

"That's stupid, but I'll can see what I can do."

"I know, I know. I tried to talk him out of it, but just talk to him. If you can."

"Ten grand, cash."

"A bit steep."

Remo says nothing. Testing how serious and/or desperate they are.

"Fine," says Alex. "I'll tell him."

"Good. Tomorrow, eleven a.m."

"Done."

Remo hangs up. Checks his wallet. He's got one credit card that belongs to his law firm, which has more than certainly been cancelled, and a personal MasterCard that may or may not have been frozen by the Feds. Might be maxed out too.

Remo doesn't like bills.

The wallet also holds two twenties and sixty-eight dollars in ones.

Remo does like strippers.

He looks around his bedroom then to his disaster of a living room. He quickly realizes he needs to find another place to lay his head for a few days. The thought also occurs to him that others might come looking for him as well. Other clients who might catch wind of the Mashburns and how Remo *handled* their case. Remo's clients don't like complications, and they also don't like lawyers who might have fucked them over.

Remo's mind clicks.

He created an *In Case of Emergency Break Glass* option a few years ago. An out. A fail-safe package. When you live the life Remo has, you need some clearly marked exits. Only problem is he created it when he was drunk out of his mind, so the location is a little fuzzy.

He spins around in a circle searching, not sure what for. His face heats quickly from a surging blood pressure spike. Fishing around the wreck that is his desk, he thinks of something. He starts looking for something very specific. Tossing papers and computer crap here and there, he digs and digs in a freakish, manic manner. His stomach drops. He starts to think he might not find what he needs. He has to find the instructions he wrote down. The instructions, more like the map, to his emergency-out option.

In disgust, he flings his laptop across the room, letting it skid-spin across the floor. He wraps his face in his hands, dropping to the floor in a heap. Panic is setting in. It's all hitting him at once. The glow of Sean is fading into the distance and the reality of what he's done is landing, punching at his insides.

Sean's face flashes into his head.

That smile.

The spark in those eyes.

Remo calms. His heartbeat returns to a normal pace. His mind slides into place, allowing his thoughts to clear. Remo bolts up, racing toward the bathroom. He lifts the lid to the tank, sliding it to the sink. Inside the toilet is a blue waterproof pouch taped inside the cool waters of the American Standard. He rips the pack off, opening it as fast as he can. With a massive exhale he removes a piece of paper from the pack.

It's a crudely drawn map with a list of instructions.

Remo's head floods with ideas. New hope. Fresh possibilities.

Maybe he can survive this.

Maybe.

As he stumbles back into the bedroom, he eyes the pile of clothes dumped on the bed.

Remo wonders, *where the fuck is my suitcase?*

3

Lester's body shakes and rattles along with the movements of the subway car.

His arms are wrapped around the suitcase he stole from Remo's closet. He lost the bat somewhere along the way, but Lester still has the important things he took from Remo's homes in New York and the Hamptons. Still has the butcher knife and the black plastic bag. Lester leans over, checks the plastic bag stuffed inside the suitcase.

The bag is important to Lester.

It contains Dutch Mashburn's head.

It's become a bit of a nasty habit for Lester, him checking the head every hour or so. He's not completely sure why he does it, either. He's stopped himself a couple of times, but sometimes he checks it without knowing he's even doing it. Like some people might nervously check their phones all the time or play with a scab. Perhaps he wants to make sure Dutch is dead. Needs to be reassured on a consistent basis. The world is a much better place without Dutch in it, that much Lester does know.

Lester is on his way back to New York City.

He believes his work is not done.

And he cannot leave with his work left undone.

He originally came to New York to save Remo. From the Mashburns, and from himself. Lester believes Remo to be a good man who needs a better man to lead him down the correct path. The path of the Lord. He is also troubled with the company Remo seems to keep.

Namely, this man called Hollis.

This Hollis is a man of violence. Lester knows it. He knows the look. It's in the eyes. The eyes tell you everything, and if you know what to look for, the eyes will spill out every damn thing you need to know about a person. The eyes Hollis has in his head scream that this is a man capable of unspeakable things.

Horrible, horrible things.

Of course, so is Lester, but that doesn't concern him at the moment.

Lester knows how to control his horrible, unspeakable side, or at least he'd like to think he does.

If Lester is to truly save Remo, then Remo cannot keep time with a man like Hollis. All of this is why Lester, former criminal, current man of the Lord, is riding on a subway dressed in a three thousand dollar suit he borrowed from Remo's closet, Bible in hand, with a suitcase containing a large butcher knife and a severed head.

4

The cab drops Remo off outside Chuck's Liquor Palace.

He just dropped off Alex's brother, Jasper, in New Jersey in an alley behind the Jiggle Queen. Jasper wanted to meet some criminals so he could do some kind of bullshit movie. A documentary, Remo thinks. Whatever. So Remo set up a meet so Jasper could try and do just that. Remo thinks it's an insane idea, but the man's money was green so, ya know, Remo's sure it'll be fine. Remo giggles to himself as he counts the ten grand Jasper paid him. A Hollywood guy mixing it up with criminals is genuinely dangerous.

However, all of this gives Remo another idea. As he cuts through the aisles containing bottle after bottle that line Chuck's Liquor Palace, Remo massages an idea. The idea movie-boy Jasper had. The core of the idea has some similarities to that of Remo's with the Mashburns. The idea of wanting to use information he holds in order to achieve another goal. Jasper the movie-boy's goals are different perhaps, but the main focus is the same. This idea actually piggybacks Remo's reasons for double-crossing the Mashburns in the first place. When that moment of

15

clarity hit Remo, it was like a freight train. Remo realized he held information that could stop some bad people from doing harm. He didn't want to sit around watching human garbage get away with hurting people.

It was really that simple.

Remo is—sorry, *was*—the best criminal defense attorney in NYC. He had an amazing list of horrible people who made up his client list. Horrible people Remo defended and won acquittals for on a routine basis.

Until the Mashburn case.

That case was different.

Very different.

Or maybe Remo was different when it hit his desk. It was after Sean was born. Regardless, Remo reviewed the case and the things the Mashburns and their crew did and something clicked. They took down a bank. Not incredibly uncommon or wretched in comparison to all the evil in the world. Remo's seen a ton of evil.

It was the way they did it.

The inhuman disregard for life.

Violent, deep wrongness.

They got their money. They didn't need to kill anyone in the bank. But boy did they. They executed every man, woman and, yes, child in that bank. Remo saw the security camera footage. Something unhinged inside his brain at that moment. Hit him between the eyes like a sledgehammer. Everything he thought he knew got turned around that day. He actually stopped and thought about people. Thought about the people being harmed by his clients. He thought of the son he had. The son he had never met. All of this swirled like a cement mixer inside Remo's jumbled head, leading him to a big decision that day. One that would change him.

Forever.

Remo decided this had to end.

He gave over everything he had on the Mashburn case to the Assistant DA. Big-ass box of evidence. Then later Remo dug up the money the Mashburns stole from the bank and gave it to charity.

Most of it.

A large percentage of it.

Come on, it was a lot of money.

Lester was part of the Mashburn crew at that time. He was the muscle. The driver. He wasn't in the bank and didn't kill anyone, on that day at least, but that day turned Lester too. Changed him. He decided things needed some change as well. The events of that day led Lester to the Lord while he was in prison. Remo wasn't willing to go that far.

Where all this plays into Remo's current state of mind is that he still doesn't like the idea these bad, bad people are out in the world and they're getting away with it all. It pisses off most people, but Remo knows he's in a different position than most people. More to the point, Remo actually knows who these bad, bad people are, and where they are.

He picks up a bottle of Johnnie Blue from the shelf.

Stops. Makes it two.

The singular idea circling round and round Remo's head is a simple one, but a difficult one to answer—*how do I stop these horrible people from doing horrible things?*

Remo spent the night at a shit motel down the street from Chuck's Liquor Palace. Before he left his place last night, he balled up all his clothes and what else he could salvage from the wreckage and dumped it into the middle of his bed. Then he wrapped the sheets around the pile and carried it out of his building, hobo-style. He carved through the onlookers and reporters in the lobby. Gave them a nice photo op, to be sure, then traveled off to the shit hotel and drank himself to sleep.

Which is why he's here now at Chuck's.

He's bone-dry.

After Remo pays for the booze, Chuck, who's working the counter, thumbs toward the back of his palace. No words spoken, none needed. It's obvious they've done this before. Often.

Stepping outside the back of Chuck's Palace and into a dirty alley, Remo looks left then right, then whistles loudly. Cats scatter. A homeless woman tells him to *shut the fuck up*. After a moment or two, out steps a young man in his early twenties. Looks like he doesn't make it out much. Hair looks like it was combed with a pillow and the bags under his eyes have bags. He hands Remo a paper bag from a pharmacy. Remo inspects the bag's contents.

"The hell is this?" asks Remo.

"Adderall. Nobody works Ritalin anymore. That's old, first generation shit."

"I like the old shit."

"Get with the times, man. Shit works the same, just an upgrade."

"Don't want a fucking upgrade, man. Didn't request a fucking upgrade. I want what I want."

"It's what I got. Give *you're welcome* a try next time."

Remo grunts then peels off some bills from the stack he got off movie-boy Jasper.

Adderall Boy's face lights up off the stack. "Wow, you see your pimp today?"

Remo turns, heads back into Chuck's. He slides into a filthy-ass bathroom. Closing the multi-stained toilet lid he takes a seat, cracks the cap and chugs some Johnnie greatness. Through his one open eye he catches a flash of a glance of himself in the cracked mirror. It's not pretty and he knows it. He just doesn't care.

Chugs harder.

Points to himself.

He starts nodding his head, as if this bottle is the correct answer to a question nobody is asking.

Yanking the bottle from his lips, letting a little bit spill on his tattered-ass suit jacket, he checks his eyes in the mirror. Needs something. Pulling the bottle of Adderall from the pharmacy bag, he pops a couple in his mouth and chases them down with Johnnie.

Satisfied with this little tune-up, he closes his eyes, leans against the questionable wall and lets the world slide together. Lets his brain come back online. Things slosh, collide, split apart and form again. For the first time in days a wave of relaxation washes over him. It's not a pure form of relaxation. More muted, but it's welcome in any form given Remo's recent history. He feels himself come down. His heart finding a normal beat. For a brief moment he's able to forget about his situation and just be. Doesn't last long. Like a lightning strike across his mind's eye he sees the Mashburns shooting everybody at the bank. The grainy security footage plays in his head like watching it for the first time.

His eyes spring open.

He pulls out the folded piece of paper that contains the instructions on where to find his *In Case of Emergency* pack. Remo knows what's in that pack, and its contents will help him to be on his way. He checks his watch, checks the instructions—he can still pick up the pack and make it to his showdown with Detective Harris at the police station.

He smiles big.

As fucked up as it is, it's all coming together Remo-style.

He thinks of Sean.

Knows he can still do some good.

Remo points, nodding at the mirror one more time.

5

The water in the pool is cold as shit.

You'd think an indoor pool would be heated for fuck's sake. Before jumping in, Remo stripped bare-ass naked. His Kiton suit is balled up in a chair with his dress socks stuffed into the toes of his slick, black Salvatore Ferragamos.

He feels his balls shrivel up into sad raisin-like nibblets.

He hears the screams from the old ladies.

Their water aerobics class has been suddenly cut short by a former big-time attorney diving into their pool with his dork swinging. Well, at the very least, it gives a slight sway.

Remo thrusts his arms in and out as hard as he can. Cutting the water. Swimming deeper and deeper like a madman to the bottom. Desperately trying to reach the floor of the deep end. He's got a Phillips screwdriver in one hand and it's hurting his ability to carve through the water like the aqua god he knows he is, but there's no other way to do this fucking thing. He curses himself for setting up the emergency pack like this. It seemed like genius at the time. Of course, at the time he was hammered out of his skull and on the downside of a two-week bender with a couple of women from Australia who dealt in the white powder game.

Good times.

After much effort, he reaches the drain cover. Manages to get one screw off before having to make a panic swim back up for air. He takes a big suck of oxygen, hears someone call him an *asshole*, then plunges back down toward the drain. This time he gets all the screws, pulls off the cover, and removes a gold key.

Exploding to the surface, Remo gasps hard, sucking in as much air as he can. He thinks he's going to die. He hasn't held his breath that long since he went down on that muscle-bound Russian lady during the Cunnilingus Incident of 2007. Holding on to the side of the pool, he can hear the insults and squawking of his new pool friends. As he pulls himself out of the pool, he realizes he's now standing in front of a pack of very angry older women. Dripping. Naked. He says nothing, allowing silence to fill the room.

He lets them stare at his member.

He simply holds his hand out, waiting.

One woman smiles big, blows him a kiss and tosses him a towel.

Remo cracks a grin, snatching the towel from the air with a snap and a wink. *Remo's still the goods, baby.*

6

The booming beat rattles Remo's teeth.

Still damp from his little dip, he stands in front of a massive brick wall across town from the pool. He clears some dirt and grime from the wall with his fingers, then tears away at strips of dark tape and removes a large sheet of cardboard. After he's finished, he can make out a clear indention in the wall. A tall rectangle. The outline of an entrance. An entrance not known by most. Remo knows that once the club inside reaches capacity someone from the place comes out and seals it up so no unwelcome guests try to join the party. Creates exclusivity to the joint, and people dig that shit.

Once this happens, you got to have a special key to get in.

Remo tosses the tape and cardboard aside. The doorway towers over him, almost mocking him and his desire to enter. Dark, gunmetal gray. There's a large goat head made of steel that stares back at him with the blackest of eyes. Inside there are the sounds of a raging party going on. Sounds like a helluva time. Muffled yelps and whoops mixed between the pounding of hip-hop thumps. He can barely make out a woman repeatedly yelling out, "Fuck yeah."

Remo leans down, getting eye to eye with the goat.

He cocks his head.

Remo thumbs the goat's nose.

He pulls out the key he retrieved from the bottom of the pool and inserts it perfectly into the goat's mouth. With a twist of the key the door creeps open on its own. The door clears a path, revealing a vision of beautiful chaos in motion. Gorgeous bodies grind and gyrate to the music blasting from an unseen sound system. The place has a high-end, trying-to-be-shitty industrial vibe going on. Nice, but not too nice. Just enough grit to be cool, but not gross. The floor is an old-school, dark hardwood with imperfections gouged and carved into it. A DJ bounces on the stage, his six-foot-plus frame silhouetted by a wall of light.

Remo stands in the doorway with his high-dollar suit that looks like hell and his moist, mussed-up hair. Looks as if he was buried alive at the bottom of a lake and has recently crawled out looking for revenge. He's painfully out of place. This is a room for the young and cool. For hot men and women with more disposable income than brain cells. One might feel self-conscious in a place like this, but not Remo. Oh no.

He owns the fucking joint.

He adjusts his collar, scans the room and says, "Excuse me, good people."

Nobody pays attention.

"Hello," he says louder.

It's like he's not even there.

He pulls his Glock from his jacket, raises it high above his head and fires a round into the ceiling.

Everything and everyone in the room freezes.

Music stops.

Gorgeous bodies become still.

"My name is Remo Cobb. This is my place. Now, in an orderly fashion, please get the fuck out."

A massive ceiling fan crashes to the floor in front of him.

Not part of Remo's plan, but he thinks the fan drop added a nice exclamation point on the thing.

————

In minutes the place is cleared out.

The DJ shuts the door and turns back to Remo, who's helping himself to a drink at the bar.

"Wish I'd known you were stopping by, man," the DJ says. "You never come here. Usually meet you at the Chinese joint."

"Came in once, remember?"

The DJ looks away. "I do."

"It was a problem, remember?"

"It was."

Remo remembers the lawsuits that stemmed from his last visit. The hospital stay. The time in a walking boot and the court-*suggested* counseling. It got ugly, man.

"Anyway, I didn't want to be able to just drop in. Just wanted the money that came off this place without having to police my self-control. It's not the greatest system, but it's a system."

"Still, I could have put something nice together for you if I'd known you were coming."

"Yeah, well, didn't know I needed to."

"What's up?"

"You like this place?"

"What? The club? Of course. It's a fucking gold mine for me and—"

"Want to buy it?"

The DJ stares at him, not sure what Remo's game is. Guy like Remo always has his game on. Remo's been good to him, but still, Remo isn't the kinda dude you trust.

"Not feelin' you," the DJ says.

"I'm having some personal issues, as well as a few legal and existential things I'm working through at the moment. I need to cut loose of some tangible items. This place being one of them. Not to mention, there's a good chance it might be taken away from me anyway."

"Yeah, I heard some heavy shit went down."

"Heavy shit indeed," Remo says. He downs his drink and moves closer to the DJ. "What do you have on you?"

The DJ blinks.

"Money. How much money do you have on you? You had to have a decent take up there tonight."

The DJ digs in his pockets, pulling out a wad of cash. Picks through the crumpled bills, a mix of tens, twenties, a Benjamin or two. "Maybe five or six hundred."

"Sold." Remo pulls a bottle of Johnnie from the bar and snatches the money from the DJ's hand.

The DJ laughs in disbelief.

"Now. Let's go in the office over there, have a drink. I'll sign the papers over to you, and then I need a few minutes alone."

"Yeah. Fuck, yeah. Anything you need. Thank you. This is amaz—"

"Is that axe still in the office?"

7

Remo uses his tie to wipe the sweat from his brow.

He brings the axe up over his head, slamming it down hard on the floor with a *thunk*. *Thunk* after *thunk* the hardwood splits and splinters, breaking off into flying pieces with each whack of the axe. Remo has been working the floor by himself like a deranged woodsman for the last hour and he's tired as hell. Soreness already setting in. He stops only long enough for a slug of Johnnie here and there. He looks to his watch. He's only got a little over an hour until his sit-down with the NYPD.

He chops and hacks away at the floor, landing the axe to the hardwood over and over again. The pain in his back and shoulders is excruciating. His muscles burn. Arms shake and vibrate. He swings harder. Faster. Face red. Snot slinging. Veins popping. A man possessed.

The axe lands with a teeth-rattling clank.

A spark fires off. Remo's eyes go wide.

He's hit metal.

Remo exhales huge, tosses the axe aside.

Dropping to his knees, he pulls and yanks with all he's got at a body-sized steel box that's stuck down in a hole in the floor. It's almost like he's dragging a coffin out from the ground. It takes everything he has left in him as he grunts and spits, working, wiggling the box up to the surface. With a final pull the box comes free, sliding through the debris onto what's left of the dance floor. Remo looks like he could puke all over the box.

He almost does.

There's a lock on the box.

"Shit."

He pats himself down, looking for a key he knows damn well he doesn't have. Thinks about pulling his gun out and shooting the damn lock off, but remembers the contents of the box and thinks better of it. He also remembers those old commercials where a lock gets shot but doesn't open. Giving the lock a hopeless tug, Remo falls back to the floor, taking a slug from his bottle.

Think.

Where the hell is that key?

His brain slides into place.

He knows where it is and it sucks.

"Shit."

8

The White Swallow is a little dead at this time of day, but there's still a reasonably sized crowd huddled at the bar.

Remo doesn't hate gays, he knows many, but he's still uncomfortable being with them and he's not sure why. So it's understandable that he's very uncomfortable being in an establishment like The White Swallow. Perhaps it's a holdover from his generation, or perhaps it's his old Texas upbringing in Cut N' Shoot. His daddy used to routinely come home from a card game drunk as hell and call Remo a *fag* or *faggot* for any variety of reasons. The reasons would stem from not taking out the trash on time to giving the old man the wrong look at the wrong time. Those and anything in between would earn a homophobic slur along with a punch or kick. People who know Remo know this about him, which is why this was a perfect place for Remo to hide something.

Rather genius when you boil it all down.

Regardless of the reasons, Remo is uneasy walking through The White Swallow en route to the bathroom. Wait. There's more to it than that. Something else is bothering Remo about being here. He can't remember what it is, but there's some serious ball of worry churning round and round in his stomach. How can his body know and fear something and his brain not have a single clue?

A chair slams into the back of his head.

Remo is launched forward, sent skidding face-first on the polished concrete floor. He flips end over end, spinning around while holding the back of his head. He looks up, fighting to find normal.

It's not here.

Not located at The Swallow.

A chair comes down hard. The legs create a small holding cell of sorts, pinning his shoulders and neck to the floor. Remo struggles briefly before realizing it's a useless exercise.

"What in the fuck, man?" Remo says.

A large wall of muscle takes a seat on the chair, now making it completely impossible for Remo to escape. Remo's eyes pop as recognition slaps him in the brain.

"Okay. Look, Mad Love, I know I owe. How much?" Remo spits out.

Mad Love simply stares down at him, picking his teeth with a toothpick. His arms are the size of thighs. His lime green T-shirt looks as if it could rip any second.

"What's the number?"

Mad Love thinks for a second while looking to the ceiling, then holds up five fingers.

"Five? That's bullshit. More like two, at best."

Mad Love chomps the toothpick between his back teeth, holds up six fingers.

"Okay. I get it. You feel that some time has passed, juice needs to be charged, and I know I've been difficult to locate—"

Seven fingers.

"Stop. Shit, motherfucker. Let me up and I'll pay you right now."

Mad Love cocks his head, birdlike. The toothpick cracks.

"Seriously. I've got it."

Mad Love gets up, removes the chair from Remo's throat, but still holds it in one fist, ready to knock the piss out of Remo if need be.

Remo stands up and pulls the envelope he got from Jasper out from his jacket. He counts out seven grand. "Still think it was bullshit that you pulled a flush that night. Granted, it was three years ago, I should move on, but you had to be a cheating little bitch. Right—"

The chair swings, knocking Remo sideways, flailing into a booth with a yelp. Remo feels his brain slosh, along with the rest of his internal organs. The impact of the chair might have literally knocked the piss out of him.

Mad Love walks over calmly and yanks the envelope from Remo's hand.

"Oh come on. That's ten damn grand. Leave me a crumb or two."

Mad Love picks through the bills and flips a single hundred-dollar bill Remo's way before walking out the door.

"Thanks," Remo mutters as he pushes himself up.

He almost passes out. His sight clouds with spots. Shaking his head violently from side to side to find his focus, he struggles to remember why the hell he came into this dump to begin with.

The bathroom.

Walking into the single-serve crapper, Remo immediately starts feeling his way behind the tank with his fingers. Panic starts to fire through him. He can't find it. His hand slaps around the back but comes up empty. He tries to jam his head between the wall and the toilet but it won't fit. He's pissed at himself for putting the key here in the first place. *Dumbass. You watched The Godfather one too many times.* After a minute or two of near hysteria, his hands frantically searching, he finds something.

A smile spreads over his busted-up face.

With a rip of tape Remo brings his hand around, holding a tiny key.

Checks his watch. It's going to be tight as hell, but he can still make it for his meeting.

A meeting with the cops.

A meeting where the main topic of conversation will be his downfall.

This time, Remo does puke.

All over himself.

9

The lock clicks open.

Remo holds his breath.

With a loud creak and some muscle strain, the metal coffin of a box opens.

Remo exhales for what seems like an hour. Relief surges through every inch of him. Inside the box is what he's been looking for. There's really not much in there, considering how big the box is, but what's in there is what is going to save Remo's moist, broken ass. He takes a pull of Johnnie while sitting on the chopped up club floor, staring at the contents. Inside the box is a brown leather overnight bag that contains the following:

Two bottles of Johnnie Blue.

And, the most important item: a portable hard drive.

Remo had every intention of putting more in the box, like money and car keys, but never got around to it. The hard drive is really all that matters, but a thinking man might have stocked an emergency pack slightly better. Remo takes a mental inventory of what's on the drive. There are about fifty gigs of documents, pics, videos and other sordid forms of digitally incriminating goodness contained on that drive. It's all there. Every bit of info in existence on every asshole criminal Remo has ever defended or come in contact with. Addresses of safe houses, aliases, detailed outlines of operations, networks, bank account numbers, and everything else a criminal can think of. All of it collected over years by him and his law firm.

A treasure chest of criminal information.

Remo created and stashed the box right after he had his moment of clarity with the Mashburn case. He wanted a life raft if the ship went down. Needed a lighthouse if (or when) a category five hurricane blew in. A survival kit with the words *in case of emergency break glass*. Or, in Remo's twisted mind, a box buried under an underground dance den with access via secret-goat-door entrance opened by a key hidden in a public pool, the survival kit key taped to the back of a crapper at The White Swallow.

It seemed reasonable at the time.

Regardless. There is a need for the contents of that box.

A need has indeed come to be, and brother…

This is one motherfucker of an emergency.

10

Remo falls into a yellow cab with the leather bag.

He clasps the bag tightly to his side, using his elbow like a vice grip.

"Nineteenth Precinct, East 67th," Remo tells the driver.

"You are covered in vomit, sir," the driver says.

"No shit."

The door opens.

A fist flies in, crunching Remo's jaw. Remo's head is sent bouncing off the far window like a racquetball. As his face springs back, the fist gives him another smack.

The door closes. A new passenger has arrived.

"You are such an asshole," Hollis says.

"East 67th?" asks the cab driver.

Hollis grunts.

The cab pulls away from the curb like it was shot from a cannon. Remo peels himself off the backseat, rubs his throbbing jaw and tries to believe what his eyes are telling him. It's Hollis and he's sitting next to him in this cab. Remo truly never thought he'd see this man again. Not after last time. Not after the shootout at the Hamptons.

"Hollis, dude," Remo says with glee. He's actually happy to see him.

Another punch.

Remo's head bounces off the window again.

The driver doesn't even look back. Too busy on his phone.

"They left, you know? My family, they packed up. They're gone," Hollis says, looking out the window. "Because of you. They left because of the shitshow you created. Cops came to my house. Threatened me. Threatened her. Now, she and my children are gone."

Remo pulls himself up in the seat next to Hollis. They stare out their respective windows, watching the city roll by. Remo's face swells. Stings like a bastard. He's taken quite a beating today. Not to mention the beating he took in the Hamptons a couple of days ago. His brief hospital stay helped, but he hasn't healed from all of that fun yet. Not by a long shot.

Remo tries to speak, but his mouth isn't working. That last pop from Hollis might have unhinged his jaw a bit. Remo rubs his face, making sure it's all there. He's not completely sure how the cops got to Hollis. Anything is possible. This is a new little wrinkle Remo was not aware of. He'll have to think about it, but later. Right now his friend, a professional killer, is highly pissed off at him.

He gives his face one last rub, resets, then says, "I'm sorry, Hollis."

Silence in the cab. Only the sounds of the city outside seep in. Remo can hear Hollis breathe. It's a slow, deep sort of breath. One of a person who's pissed off and thinking very hard about why he's pissed off. Remo braces himself for another punch that he's sure is coming his way.

"Yeah, I'm sure you're sorry as hell," Hollis says, buried in his own thoughts.

Remo knows he's right. About it all being his fault. Can't argue it. Remo begged Hollis to help him with the Mashburns when he visited Hollis at his home in the burbs. Practically guilted the man into it. Make no mistake, without Hollis's help Remo would be dead as Dillinger. No question about that. Hollis is the toughest person Remo has ever known. The things he's seen and heard about the hitman, it's a scary-ass resume for sure. A killer in every sense of the word. A professional killer with a family he loves and would burn down the entire city to protect. Now they've left him. His wife went bye-bye in order to protect their children.

Now, this man who saved his ass is broken.

All because of Remo.

Remo looks to his leather bag on the floor of the cab.

"I've got a plan, if that helps," he says. "In that bag is something that could get us to free and clear."

Hollis says nothing, still lost inside his head, staring out the window.

"No, really. I think I can get this mess cleared up. You gotta believe me, I had no idea they were going after you and the family."

"Yeah."

"I didn't. Really."

"Yeah."

"Dammit. It's true. I would never put your family at risk—"

Remo's cell goes off. He glances to the screen. It's Anna, his ex-wife.

"Shit." Remo turns to Hollis. "I gotta take this."

"Yeah."

Remo's eyes roll. He's got sympathy for the man, but Hollis's little pity party is starting to get old.

"Anna?"

"Hey. Look, I fought even calling you, but Sean wanted to see if you're okay."

Remo's busted-up face lights up. "He did? That's great."

"Yes, Remo, it's great that our son is wondering if you're okay after seeing on TV that his father was knee-deep in a bloodbath. It's simply fucking fantastic."

"Okay, fine. Does he want to talk?"

"He does, but he's not here." Anna sighs. "Remo, try to grasp what I'm about to say. This… situation is a lot for a little boy to take in. You. Meeting you. What's going on with you. To be honest, it's a lot for me."

"Anna—"

"Shut up and listen. He wants to get to know you. Of course he does." She sounds as if she's working it out as she speaks. "It's probably not horrible if he actually knows his father. Even if it is you. In a limited, monitored capacity of course. Very limited. As in not much. Tiny amount is best."

Her end of the call goes quiet. Remo's not sure what he's supposed to do here. "Let me know when I can speak."

"Shut. Up. I need to think about this, okay? I just— I don't know the best way to go with this."

Remo's stomach flutters. This is what he wanted all along, even if he didn't know it. His brain didn't connect the dots before, but this is what he was really going for when he got involved with all the unfortunate business with the Mashburns. Before, he only thought he wanted to meet Sean before he died, but what he really wants is to be a part of his son's life. If only a small part.

He wants to be a dad.

He realizes he'll never be a dad in the traditional sense. That ship has sailed, and let's be honest, Remo ain't the sort. Not to mention, Anna would rather drink gasoline and shove a match up her ass than reconcile with Remo. Regardless of all of this, Remo can't help but smile.

He looks to Hollis.

He's not smiling.

He's broken. Broken because of Remo. Remo's smile fades.

"You listening to me? Asshole, hello?" says Anna.

"Of course. Take all the time you need to think about it. I'm open to whatever you want to do."

Anna goes silent. She's not sure what to do with an agreeable, rational Remo. "Okay," she says, and hangs up.

Remo pockets his phone while fighting to control his happiness. He's practically bouncing in the seat. Remo's learned over the years that irrational exuberance can lead to some hairy-assed issues. His mom died when he was young and his father wasn't a big fan of showing his happy side, at least not in front of Remo. Dad was more than happy to show his pissed-off, drunken-rage side, however. Yet, despite this, Remo can't help but smile wide. He looks to his bag again. His plan B. His emergency pack and, brother, this is an emergency. Breaking the damn glass on this thing is the only plan. It's flimsy, this little hope of his, this plan Remo is cooking up for his meeting with the cops, but this shit has to work. Now more than ever.

For Remo.

For Hollis.

For Sean.

11

Remo sits staring into the abyss.

Staring at Detective Harris.

They are on opposite sides of a beaten-to-hell metal table in a room located at the back of the 19th Precinct. Not an attractive room by any stretch. Not supposed to be. Movies and TV have captured its essence pretty well actually. Neutral-colored, bare walls. Nothing to write home about and not a room you'd like to hang out in. Damn bleak. No conversation starters in here. Nothing to distract the occupants from the task at hand, and that task is the cops extracting from your head what you know as quickly as possible.

To be clear, Remo and Harris hate each other.

Not a garden-variety hate either. Not a casual misunderstanding or an argument over blah blah. This is the sort of hate that bubbles and builds over years and years. Years and years of Remo setting criminals free. Criminals Harris and his fellow officers worked damn hard to apprehend. Some of the worst scum New York has ever produced and Harris knows this slick-as-shit lawyer has made a mountain of money defending them.

Remo doesn't have a real reason to hate Harris. He simply hates Harris because Harris hates him. Perhaps not the healthiest way to live, but it's what keeps a guy like Remo plowing through this thing called life. He feeds off the hate of others, thus feeding his own hate and propelling him headlong into questionable decisions at a blinding rate of speed. Again, not recommended, but it's better than living a passionless life. At least that's how Remo sees it.

There's a shit-ton of history between these two and none of it is good. Remo has a convenient way of forgetting history as it happens. More efficient than therapy. Harris, however, digs his fingernails into history and holds on for dear life. Like clinging to the rim before the big flush. It's all he's got. Strangely, the hate is also what keeps a guy like Harris plowing through as well.

But that's all history.

Today they are in the here and now.

The right now.

The two men sit staring at one another without saying a single word. They've been like this for a solid hour. Seriously, a whole hour. Two stubborn assholes sitting eyeballing the hell out of each other. Hate flung back and forth without a word spoken. Remo is screaming inside. Not showing it, but this whole thing is killing him. The silence is making his skin crawl. He wants to get to his plan and get the hell on with his life. He knows this whole unfortunate mess can be cleared up lickety–split if Harris will tap out of prick mode long enough to hear him out.

"Fuck this," Remo mutters to himself, hits reset then throws a toothy grin at Harris. "How ya been, brutha?"

Harris picks his teeth with his thumbnail, sucking in whatever he just jarred loose.

"Last time I saw you I almost got killed. If memory serves," Remo says.

"Which time?"

"Pardon?"

"Which time you almost got killed? I saw you at the Chinese joint after your boy, Lester, got shot up and you hit the floor like a pussy. That was kinda cool, by the way. Actually, the last time I saw you wasn't that long ago. It was in the hospital after you almost bought it in the Hamptons. Some pissed off, piece-of-shit clients you fucked over stopped by to execute your sorry fucking ass. So, I'll ask again: which time are you talking about?"

Now Remo picks his teeth with his thumb. "Doesn't matter."

"No, it does not." Harris goes back to staring.

Remo raps his fingers on the table. He was hoping the booze would even him out, but he's still jumpy. Hollis, along with Remo's brown leather bag from the club floor, is waiting for Remo at a bar not far from here. He trusts Hollis with it. Not because Remo has any kind of deep trust in his fellow man. It's more because he explained his plan to Hollis and Hollis doesn't really have a choice other than to wait and see how this shakes out. Self-preservation. That much Remo trusts.

Remo raps the table faster. The beat he's playing might be Metallica.

"Please stop that shit," Harris says.

"Are we waiting for something?"

"We are."

"What, exactly? Love to get the hell on with this."

Harris clears his throat then smiles big. "The CIA wants a word."

43

"CIA?"

"Yup. They're kinda dicks about things. If memory serves."

"What do they want?"

"Seems you've stepped in it, Slick."

"Perhaps I did." Remo takes moment, then says, "Or did they think you'd fuck everything up?"

Harris's stare changes ever so slightly. There's a flash to his eyes. Only a flicker, not much of anything most people would notice, but it's enough for a guy like Remo to dig his claws into.

"Holy shit. That's it. You and your merry little band of dumbshits can't be trusted with the Hamptons shootout. Lots of media on it. Very high profile, right? Needs to done correctly, as in really correctly. That's it, right?"

Remo keeps hammering away at the red-faced, shaking-with-anger Harris.

"Big, bad Detective Harris and his NYPD blue balls can't be trusted to handle something as open and shut as a luxury neighborhood bloodbath. Damn, that's gotta sting."

A man standing behind Remo says, "You're incorrect, Remo."

Harris face turns white as he whispers, "Agent Cormack."

Remo turns, finding Cormack leaning in the doorway. Dark suit. Short, tight hair. Fit as fuck with blue eyes that carve through you. A special agent man right out of central casting.

"Not correct at all. Is it, Detective Harris?" Cormack asks.

Remo looks to Harris. The good detective acts as if his mom just came home early and caught him jerking off. He curls up into a ball of confusion. A frozen-faced, twisted mix of terror and shame. He's no longer the tough New York cop from a few moments ago. No, not even close. Remo has never seen anything like it. He'd take some joy in watching Harris sweat like this if it wasn't for the fact he's more than a little concerned that the CIA is involved in this whole mess. Given that the CIA's primary area of focus is foreign threats and Remo's primary area of focus is domestic assholes, Remo is his own private ball of confusion. This is something he did not plan for.

Never occurred to him.

Why would it?

"Why does the CIA give two shits about me?" Remo asks.

Cormack shrugs off the question as he steps into the room. He pauses, then leans down so he can speak into Remo's ear. "Let's talk. Doesn't have to be a big thing. I want you to be comfortable. We'll head over to your favorite Chinese place. Cool with you?"

Remo turns to face Cormack.

"*Yes* is the word you're hunting for, Remo."

Remo nods.

Cormack nods.

Remo swallows hard.

Cormack pokes Remo on the nose while making a *boop* sound.

Remo needs a drink.

12

The Asian waitress drops off a mug of coffee, along with a big-as-your-face plate of chicken fried rice.

Remo and CIA Agent Cormack sit at Remo's favorite table. The one three tables down from the entrance and three up from the back of the restaurant. It has a big, nice window that looks out upon the buzzing streets of the city. A front-row seat to the twirling soup of humanity that is New York. Remo comes here most nights to get away. To think. To step out of whatever mood-altering sandbox he's been playing in that day. Watching people out the window calms him, much like watching the ocean calms other people. There's something about watching them all move to a path and rhythm only known by them. Driven by meeting a friend, a hot date, late for whatever, an important appointment with who knows. Got to get home to the kid. Got to get to the store. Get to work. Get a job. Get home before they pass out face-first in the gutter.

Endless possibilities.

Remo watches them all. Watches them move through their lives, all through his window to the world. A window that has been recently replaced by the restaurant. A window that a troubled member of the Mashburns known as Chicken Wing shot out while Remo sat at this very table enjoying the same meal with another man. A man named Lester. During that meal, Remo dove from the booth, hit the floor—as Detective Harris mentioned—and Lester was the one who caught the bad side of that deal. He took a bullet, or was it bullets?

Remo was positive Lester was dead that day.

He wasn't.

"Eat up, man. My treat," Cormack says.

Remo can only look at his steaming plate of rice with chunks of chicken fighting for real estate along with cubes of carrots and the tiny peas. He is hungry, but doesn't want to give any power to Cormack. If Remo took a bite right now, that would come off as Remo taking orders. Putting Cormack in the position of giving orders and Remo in the position of taking them. In Remo's world this is also known as bending over and letting them do what they want with you. Of course there's little doubt Cormack holds every ounce of power in this situation, but Remo would rather not make it so damn obvious, or bend over for Cormack's wants and desires.

"Here." Cormack pulls a small flask from his jacket and pours some familiar brown liquor into Remo's coffee. "That's better. Johnnie Walker Blue, correct?"

Remo wants to jump out of his skin.

1. That is exactly how Remo likes his coffee. Looks soooo good.
2. How does this prick know this?
3. Fuck. Fuck. Fuckity. Fuck. Fuck.

Cormack picks up a spoon and stirs Remo's coffee. "Now, I'm a *cards on the table* kind of dude. I own your buddy, Detective Harris. I'm sure you know this already, but in case you don't, he's in one hell of a mess." Cormack taps the coffee off the spoon using the edge of the cup, then wipes the spoon down with a red napkin. "Not an original story—cop with a gambling debt, hooker troubles, you know the sort. And I've got him on all of it. Could have buried him deep. Could have taken down half his department, but I didn't. Didn't want that. I wanted to trade up. You know why?"

Remo's stomach drops through the floor.

It's the look on Cormack's face.

This guy is in complete control and he knows it. Remo knows the feeling and the look that comes along with it. A feeling that comes from absolute confidence. The look Cormack has right now and the feeling that's more than likely surging through him is one Remo's experienced many, many times. In interrogation rooms. In courtrooms. Bars. Bedrooms. It's a feeling like you've got a bomb in your back pocket that only you know about, and you're just waiting to shove it up someone's ass.

Remo picks up his coffee, taking a long sip, trying hard not to show his shaking hands.

"Don't know?" Cormack asks. "Give up?"

Remo gives a single nod.

"I traded up for you. You, Remo. That has to make you feel special, correct?"

"Special?" asks Remo.

"Yes."

"Not correct."

"Yeah, I gave up all the things I could've done to Harris and his people, and it would have been a blast, to be sure, but I passed all that up to get here. To this place here and now to get to you."

Now Remo eats his rice. Feels like a last-supper type of thing now.

"Now. You're thinking, what's he got? What's this CIA a-hole holding? I'll tell you. I'll lay down my cards for you to look at. Nothing to hide, Remo. Does that interest you?"

Remo drinks some more from his juiced-up coffee mug. His brain spins. Flips. Catches fire. He's still got his emergency pack. His hard drive. His own smart bomb that'll get him out of this. Remo just needs to keep this ego-driven, civil servant fuckstick talking. Let him rant and give up everything. Then Remo will rain down some wrath-of-God-level shit matched by no man.

"I'll help you out, Remo. I'll keep talking and give up all I've got so you can have time to think. I know that's what you're doing. It's the smart way to play this, and you're a smart dude. I like that about you. The more I talk, the more I give, the more time you get to think and counterattack what I've got. I went to law school too."

Remo runs his tongue across his teeth and leans back into the booth.

"This is fun." Cormack smiles. "Okay. What I've got is video of you and your friend Hollis at multiple stoplights, at a gun store trying out several guns and working over a firing range like weekend warriors in training, and then I've got you buying mattresses and tootling down the aisles of Home Depot."

Remo glances to the door, thinks of running away.

"All of the items in those videos? From the gun store, the

mattresses and the cart full of crap you guys bought at Home Depot? I say crap and items—right now they're considered 'evidence.' All of that matches the items-slash-evidence found in the house in the Hamptons. The house that was covered in blood and bodies. Blood and bodies of your clients in a house you own."

Remo thinks of jamming his fork into Cormack's eye.

Cormack slides Remo's knife and fork away and over to his side of the table. "All of that suggests you knew what was going down. Prepared for something, perhaps set a trap. Perhaps premeditated murder. Who knows, but you could make an argument, correct?"

Remo wishes Chicken Wing would come back and shoot him.

"You take all that and mix in the possibility that you threw your case against the Mashburns. Ya know, the same Mashburns who were found shot all to hell in your Hamptons getaway? Plus, oh yeah, your friend Hollis is a known hitman. You can see how this doesn't look great for you. Or Hollis."

Remo's eyes go wide. Now the CIA is threatening Hollis. It's one thing to go after Remo like this, but Hollis has already been through enough because of him. Now Cormack is the one being silent. Waiting. Waiting for Remo's move.

Remo coughs. "I have something, too."

"Do tell."

"I need to know we can talk."

"We are talking."

"Need to know we can talk a deal. A real deal, not some reduced blah blah horseshit. A deal where me and Hollis walk with hands clean."

"Your and Hollis's hands will never be clean. You know that. I can't help you with that, not in a spiritual or moral sense. I can put on my listening ears and hear what you have to say, and if what you have to say is worth anything, then I'll consider almost anything."

"It's worth quite a bit."

"Sounds fantastic."

"It is."

"Can't wait."

Remo takes a gulp of coffee, takes in a deep breath and says, "I've got a hard drive that contains extensive evidence that can put away every client I or my firm has ever worked for."

Cormack simply blinks.

He doesn't even bother changing his expression.

Part II

Something drastic.

13

Remo stares back at Cormack.

The man hasn't said anything for at least a full minute. Remo can't tell if this is good or bad, but he won't give Cormack the satisfaction of asking. He'll sit here a fucking week if he has to.

"That it?" Cormack asks.

"It's a lot."

"It is, no doubt, but it's pretty useless to me."

Remo feels his guts crank. "Useless?"

"Remo, you know damn well I can't use anything from you in court."

"I have everything. Bank accounts. Safe houses. Names and addresses of girlfriends, of boy toys, of everything these fuckers are involved in. All you have to do is say you uncovered it at the house in the Hamptons."

"All good stuff. And you'll probably need it all."

Remo stops, leans forward, doesn't like what he just heard.

Cormack pours another snort of Blue into Remo's coffee. "That's right. *You* will need them."

"*You* might need to clarify that."

"I will. It's great you and I are on the same page. I was thinking more or less the same thing you were, only with a slightly different twist. When I heard you fucked over the Mashburns and that you gave away the money to charity, most of it at least, I was inspired."

Remo looks away, a little sheepish.

"It gave me an idea. That the biggest asshole defense attorney in New York, a guy who has access to the dirty deeds of so many other assholes, can be very, very helpful to me. Especially if that asshole defense attorney has had a crisis of conscience, has struggled with the morality of his work."

"Where is this going?"

"You're going to use what you know, what's on that hard drive and whatever else you've got, to help me take care of some very bad guys and gals."

Remo laughs.

Cormack laughs harder.

Remo tries to top the intensity and volume of Cormack's laughter.

The restaurant looks on with great discomfort.

Cormack goes louder and harder.

It's getting ridiculous.

They wind down to a stop.

"How?" asks Remo.

"How what?"

"I don't understand what you want me to do."

"Simple, really. You are going to continue what you started with the Mashburns. You're going to help rid the earth of horrible people."

Remo rules out the idea Cormack is a mind reader and read his thoughts earlier about doing that very thing. It was fine when it was Remo's idea. When it was Remo's choice. But this is fucked up.

"I'm sorry, I should have been more clear. That Mashburn thing was a onetime deal," Remo says.

"Nope."

"I'm not a trained killer."

"Easy now. Didn't say anything about killing, but if some dead bad guys pop up I won't hate you for it."

"You're insane."

"Nope. I'm not."

"How do you propose I do this?"

"I'm not going to tell you your business, Remo. Get creative. You might start with Hollis though. He's a five-star badass from what I understand."

"We're not the fucking Avengers."

"Of course not, that would be ridiculous. Love those movies though. No, you just need to figure out how to keep doing what you started. How to keep doing good." Cormack picks up the check and slides out from the booth. "I gotta bounce, man. I've enjoyed this, but I want to make sure I leave you with a clear understanding of what we've been talking about here. You will do this, or I will burry you and Hollis under a prison of my choosing. Got it?"

Remo nods.

"Good." Cormack makes it about two steps then snaps his fingers, spinning around. "Oh, one last thing. Mr. Crow."

"What about him?"

"He's a client of yours, and a disease. I'd like you to remove him from circulation."

14

Remo walks into the joint where Hollis sits waiting.

Hollis sits at the bar about halfway through a beer that's larger than his shoe. An empty shot glass also rests in front of him with a mangled lime laid out like a twisted body thrown from a car. He glances up to Remo. He can see it all over him. Hollis doesn't like it, and he doesn't want to hear Remo's bullshit.

"Fuck," Hollis says.

Remo takes a stool next to him, taking note of his brown leather bag resting on the other stool. He motions to the bartender to set them up with another round.

"It's not that bad."

"You're so full of shit," Hollis says.

"Okay, fine. We're fucked."

"Which prison are we going to?"

"Not prison I'm concerned with."

"Oh? Firing squad?"

"Kinda."

This catches Hollis's attention.

The bartender delivers two fresh beers and two tequila shots with salt and lime. Remo holds up a finger, requesting a moment from Hollis. He raises his shot, clinks it with the one waiting for Hollis. Hollis glances to Remo, trying to guess where this conversation is going. Deciding that's a fool's errand, Hollis picks up his shot with a nod as the two old *friends* throw them back at the same time. Like synchronized swimming for the drunk and despondent. After destroying his lime, Remo empties his beer in three gulps.

"We have to *take down* some bad guys," Remo says.

"Define *take down*." Hollis pauses. "Better define *bad guys*, too."

"Bad gals, too."

"Need a definition there, too."

"I'm a little fuzzy on both, to be honest. CIA is involved however—"

"I'm sorry, CIA? We going after terrorists?"

"There's this agent named Cormack. Real fuckin' ballbuster. This guy, this fucking guy didn't want my hard drive but wants us to use the info on it and whatever else we've got to..." Looks skyward, searching for the words. "Let me make sure I say this right, *to take Mr. Crow out of circulation*."

"What the hell does that even mean?"

"You're the slick-ass hitman, was hoping you knew that type of talk."

"He wants us to hunt and kill Crow?"

"That's what was implied. He never really said kill anybody."

Now Hollis empties his beer in a minimal amount of gulps. Remo gives an air circle to the bartender for another round. They sit with their thoughts churning, both pretending to watch volleyball on ESPN.

"I'm running," says Hollis.

"It's the CIA, man."

"Outrun them before."

"Not like this."

"Why *not like this*?"

"They've got video. Video of you, with me, loading up for war right before the Hamptons, and they found it all after we ran the hell away. That's why they went to your wife and kids, I'm guessing. More of a message to you. They want you to know they will hunt you and your family down."

Bartender delivers the new round. Hollis takes his shot alone this time then grunts out, "Fucking hate you."

"Fine."

"This is all your fucking fault. I had to rush through shit to keep your sorry ass alive. If I had time I would have planned this out the right way. I was forced into being sloppy because of your dumbass, and now I'm fucked. Completely fucked because of you."

"I feel horrible."

"You don't feel shit."

Remo shrugs, then throws back his shot.

The two *friends* drain their beers in perfect harmony without bothering to look at each other. Remo knows Hollis doesn't have any great options with this situation. None that are realistic at least. Technically Hollis doesn't even exist. He's a ghost. The life he's been living is a complete fabrication. His neighbors know him as Bob. Bob plays golf, grills his special pork chops on Saturday, goes to church and helps out at the kids' school whenever needed. Hollis, however, kills people all over the world for a price. A steep price. He's got the dual life thing down cold. Dead-solid perfect. Only problem is that because Bob isn't truly real, everything that *is* real is in his wife's name. The house. The bank and brokerage accounts. Credit cards. All of it. She's real. Real as shit and she's really pissed with Hollis. So pissed she took it all and went gone baby gone leaving Bob/Hollis with three hundred twenty-six dollars and a budding depression that's teetering on an institutional-grade mindfuck.

"I should just shoot you. Dump your carcass. Leave town immediately. Boom, problem solved," Hollis says.

"Those are options, I guess."

"Yes, yes they are."

"And?"

"Nothing is off the table."

"I'm here all day."

A man steps up behind them and speaks. "Excuse me. This seat taken?"

Remo turns. "No…"

Lester cocks his head and gives Remo a finger-curl wave.

Hi.

15

Remo falls off his stool.

Ass hits the tile.

Hollis fires off his stool, sending it slamming into the bar, bouncing off about a foot and a half. He's on his feet, ready to roll. In the blink of an eye Hollis is in beast mode, ready to take Lester's head off. A highly trained instrument of mayhem that's itching to release.

Lester widens his stance, squares his shoulders, but doesn't look all that concerned. Lester lacks Hollis's skills, but he's no stranger to violence. He might not know advanced combat tactics or the sweet, subtle art of hand-to-hand, but Lester has been fighting his whole life. In the streets, in the prisons and everywhere else he's ever been. A lifetime of self-taught survival training that's provided a lifetime scars to prove it.

Remo fumbles getting to feet. His face is a mangled mess of freshly-made confusion and pain. The fall from the stool really hurt his ass, but Lester standing here is almost as painful.

"Lester. What the hell are you doing here?" asks Remo.

"Felt like I was needed after all that unfortunate business at your beach home." He looks to Hollis. "It's this one, really. He was with you, right? There's something about him. Something ugly."

"Did he really just call me ugly?" Hollis asks.

"Not your appearance, friend." Lester smiles. "It's all in your eyes. There's violence behind them. More like your soul that's in disrepair. Much like our mutual friend here, Remo. You need some light too." Lester takes a step closer to Hollis. "Do you wish Remo harm?"

"Of course I do. Everyone who's ever met him wishes him harm."

Lester can't help but chuckle at that one. It's the truth that makes it funny.

Remo waves his hands at Hollis, trying to get his attention. Trying to let him know Lester is a delicate touch and to stop rolling down whatever road Hollis is about to roll down. These are difficult concepts to get across with a simple hand wave, but it doesn't stop Remo from giving it a shot. He adds a whistle to the mix. Doesn't work.

Lester steps even closer to Hollis, just shy of nose to nose. "Tell me I'm wrong about you. Tell me I'm imagining the things I see when I look at you, because I don't think I am."

"No, I think you're seeing me just fine."

Remo attempts to worm his way between them but fails miserably. He jams a hand between them in a feeble attempt to separate the two war machines. Nothing. They don't move, not an inch. Remo tries with two hands. Nothing. It's as if he's trying to separate two trucks that are parked too close together.

Remo rubs his face in a quick, frantic motion. Completely

frustrated, Remo resets, takes a deep breath. "How about a drink, Lester? On me. On your old buddy Remo." Looks Lester up and down. "Is that my fucking suit?" He glances to Lester's side. "My suitcase too? Damn it, man."

Lester doesn't bother looking Remo's way. His focus is squarely on Hollis and Hollis is zeroed in on Lester. Hollis has already decided how he's going to kill him. Using previsualization, Hollis has already mapped it all out. He'll start with snapping Lester's right kneecap with his heel then put Lester on the floor with a tomahawk elbow strike to the nose. Once he's down, Hollis will stomp his nuts then finish God Boy off with a snap of the neck.

Lester hasn't mapped it out, but he knows that he'd enjoy making Hollis bleed. Some screaming and begging might be nice as well.

Two warriors toe to toe.

Neither one backing down.

Both prepared to destroy.

Remo knows what these men are capable of. He's seen them both in action, seen them both when they are on fire, and it scares the shit out of him. As much as he'd love to witness this clash of the titans, Remo knows a public bloodbath isn't going to help anyone. They will either both be dead, one of them will be dead and the other will be dying, or worse. In Remo's mind, the worst-case scenario is Remo dying while trying to stop them from killing each other. Also, there's a far-greater-than-zero chance the cops would end up being called, if they haven't been contacted already. There's no upside here. No one is going to win this thing.

"Look, people—friends. We can't do this. We need to stick together," Remo says. His words don't seem to land with either of them. Remo works another angle. "We, the three of us, have some common ground here," Remo presses. "You're fucked up with Jesus, you're fucked up with family shit, and I'm just fucked up. We're the same, when you think about it."

Not even a glance.

This unresponsive behavior upsets Remo more than anything. He thought that last one was a pretty good line.

There's a wave of coldness that seems to slide across Hollis's eyes. Remo's seen it before, and it wasn't a good thing. Looking to Lester, Remo sees nothing. Blank, dark eyes that simply do not care about what happens to him or to Hollis.

This is about to go off. Remo has to do something.

Something drastic.

Something to defuse the situation and give him a chance to talk some sense into these two masters of disaster. Remo holds his breath, then does that *something*.

Remo jams his hands down their pants.

One down the front of Lester's, one down the front of Hollis's.

Remo grabs ahold of their balls, hanging on for dear life. Using the hardest grip he can, Remo clamps his right hand on Hollis's jewels and uses his left to take hold of Lester's hairy set of pills. As if milking two cows at the same time.

Both Lester's and Hollis's eyes pop wide.

Bulge huge.

There's some coughing. Red faces. Lip biting. Teeth grinding. After the initial wave of shock and nausea passes, they both look to Remo, who stands there holding on as if he were competing in a psychopath rodeo.

Remo gives his best apologetic tone. "Look. I'm sorry. I need to talk to both of you like civilized human—"

Lester and Hollis both whip guns out.

Hollis jams the barrel of his gun into Remo's right eye. Lester takes the left. Remo still holds on to his boys' balls. He can feel them there, he just can't see what he's doing with guns blocking his field of vision.

"Okay," Remo says, "I know this is awkward for all of us, but let's think this through."

"Let. Go. Of my balls," Hollis says.

"Yes, Remo. Stop doing that," Lester says.

The bar has already cleared out. Remo's more than fairly sure the bartender has called the cops by now.

He swallows hard. "Look. Let's think, talk it out together. We are in a public place. There are men with guns drawn and balls are in custody. The cops will be here any second. What exactly are we going to tell them?"

Lester and Hollis glance to one another.

Both their faces red as hell.

Sweat drips.

"Think, boys. How does getting arrested right now help any of us?" Remo hopes his words are taking hold this time. He can't see, so he can't get a read on their faces. Can only hope that self nut-love and common sense can cut through the anger of two violent-as-hell men.

Lester removes his gun.

Hollis follows suit.

Remo blinks his vision clear, then releases their sacks.

16

Remo washes his hands.

He decided to make an upgrade on his living arrangements. He's moved on to the Essex House located Midtown across from the park. It was a bit of a gamble, using his Amex to get the room, considering there's a chance the powers that be had frozen his account, but once it cleared he asked for a penthouse that had a nice view of the city he loves. Considering he might be dead or in prison soon, he figured why not live a little?

Besides, he wanted a nice place to have a meeting.

A meeting of dangerous minds.

Lester and Hollis are seated on a plush couch looking out over Central Park. Hollis holds a glass of vodka on the rocks. Lester holds his leather-bound Bible and a bottle of whiskey. Neither one looking at the other. Eyes forward. Still not happy.

Still considering killing one another.

Remo steps out from the bathroom, wiping his hands dry with a hotel towel. He stands behind them and can only see the backs of their heads, but he can feel the anger radiating from the couch.

He takes a moment to look out the window, soaking in the view. *It really is a great park,* he thinks. Massive, sprawling, peppered with every walk of life imaginable, coming from everywhere possible. Lifelong New Yorkers, tourists, immigrants fleeing a third world shithole, transplants fleeing a small-town US shithole, and whatever else you can think of. Most chasing a dream or just looking for a better life. Remo's thoughts drift to Sean and Anna.

Are they out there right now?

In the park, enjoying the day?

Remo hopes so.

He hopes Sean is running and playing with all he has. Hopes Sean will play as long and as hard as he can, because one day that will stop. One day Sean will be an adult with adult problems and all the horrible shit that goes along with it. He will more than likely never have to deal with the issues his father has had to work through. At least Remo hopes to hell he won't.

Remo hopes Sean will never have to grab two killers by the balls.

"You might have pulled one loose," Hollis says, rubbing himself.

Remo smirks, then pours himself a glass of water. He needs to lay off the sauce, at least for a bit. He does need to focus, however. He pops a pill. Taking a seat in a cushy-ass chair across from the couch, Remo looks over his people. His new team. His new marriage, of sorts.

Lester, Hollis and Remo.

For better or worse.

"How the fuck did we end up here?" Remo asks.

"You're an asshole, that's how," says Hollis.

"He's not wrong, actually." Lester nods while rubbing his Bible. "You are the link to both of us and you being, pardon the expression, an *asshole* is the reason I'm here. Solid. Can't argue with it, man."

Hollis and Lester share a nod, perhaps common ground.

"Okay, regardless." Remo stands, pacing back and forth in front of the window. "We share a problem. Right?"

"Yeah. You," Hollis says.

Lester nods.

"What I mean is regardless of how or why we got here, we have the same problem and that problem is the CIA, the cops and whatever the fuck else wants to own us." Remo turns to Lester. "You might still be able to bolt, man. Cormack didn't say anything about you."

Lester cocks his head. "Cormack? What's a Cormack?"

Hollis leans over. "CIA dude that has a hard-on for Remo."

Lester nods, then motions for Remo to continue.

Remo goes on. "You can probably break free of us and whatever shit we're knee-deep into."

"I came back to help you, Remo," Lester says. "I made a decision to save you and you are far, far from saved. The Lord placed me with you. Twice now. I see that now more than ever."

Hollis looks over at Lester's suitcase, noticing something.

"Lester. Man, come on."

"Remo, you did an amazing thing for me. You saved me much in the same way. Even if you didn't realize you were doing it. You risked everything with the Mashburns. You put me, and them, in prison. Forced me to take moment. A cleansing moment. In the

69

process you set me free. Don't you see that? Can't you see that is something I can't simply walk away from?"

"I guess, but shit, dude."

Hollis squints, trying to get a better look at the suitcase. There's something that looks a lot like hair peeking out from the zipper of Lester's, really Remo's, suitcase. He gets up, walking toward it while Remo and Lester continue their conversation.

"*You guess?*" Lester says. "That's what is so endearing about you, Remo. You don't even know the good in you. I know what people say about you, and perhaps it's all true, but I see the light in you, and brother, it's bright."

Hollis reaches the suitcase.

"And if you don't realize that light that's inside you, if you don't know that about yourself, that's okay. I see it. The Lord sees it. So if you don't mind, I'd like to stay and help you through this fucked up shit."

Remo feels his eyes water a bit. He's hit with an odd moment of emotion, hearing Lester's words. The fact Lester would pledge his life, not to get all *Lord of the Rings* with this, but in a way Lester is pledging his sword for Remo, is damn touching.

Remo extends his hand to Lester.

Lester grabs it and brings Remo in tight for a massive, bone-crushing hug.

All air escapes Remo's body as Lester squeezes tighter and tighter. Lester speaks into Remo's ear. "I'm not going anywhere, brother. We'll get through this, okay?"

Remo grunts out, "Okay."

"What. The. Fuck?" Hollis barks.

Lester releases Remo. They turn to find Hollis holding Dutch

Mashburn's severed head in the air by the hair. Hollis's eyes are wide as plates, looking directly at Remo.

Remo has nothing to say. With his mouth wide open, his eyes slip over to Lester.

Lester shrugs.

"Lester, amigo. We need to lose that head," Remo says.

"I disagree."

"Lester. Dump Dutch's melon."

Dejected, Lester snatches the head from Hollis's grip. With the head swinging by his hip, Lester looks around, then drops it in a trash can next to the desk by the window.

Hollis is in complete disbelief. He runs his hand through his hair. "You can't put it in the trash." He spins toward Remo. "Who the fuck is this guy?"

"Lester, he's right. This room is in my name. Someone might notice a severed head in the trash."

"Then what?" asks Lester.

Remo looks out the window. He presses his forehead against the glass, looking out toward the park, letting the coolness of the window offer some form of comfort in this moment of madness.

Lester's confused. "We can't throw it out that way. Window doesn't open."

Hollis rolls his eyes.

Remo continues to watch the park, wishing he was there and not here. Wishing he was actually anywhere but here. He pivots his face toward Lester, keeping his forehead on the glass. "No, man. We'll go down to the park and find a dumpster or something. They find severed shit in the park all the time."

"Fine, fuck it," Lester says in a huff, jamming Dutch's head back into the suitcase. There's an ear still sticking out.

"Oh for fuck's sake." Hollis moves Lester out of the way, stuffing the head deep into the suitcase himself.

Lester shoves Hollis away from the suitcase.

Hollis shoves Lester back. Looks like two school kids seconds away from a slap fight.

"Hey," Remo barks. "Want me to start snagging nuts?"

The two stop like brothers scolded by a fed-up parent.

"Good. Lets dump that nasty-ass head and figure out how to get un-fucked."

17

Lester shoves his arm shoulder-deep into a Central Park trash can.

Remo and Hollis stand in front of him, attempting to shield Lester from view.

Hollis is quiet, casting a silent stare across the park.

Remo's mind cranks at a thousand thoughts per second.

Lester hums a church hymn.

"Got it yet, God Boy?" asks Hollis.

Lester ignores the jab as he pushes Dutch's head farther and farther into the can. Through the half-eaten hot dogs and ice treats. Past the bags of dog shit, the discarded napkins and the pounds of city waste.

Remo thinks of Crow.

Mr. Crow. Cormack's target.

Remo's client.

A former client who lives the good life of a NYC crime god. Crow enjoys two things, really. Money and his little side hobby of murdering prostitutes. Crow was Remo's client for years, one of his first actually. He started out as a small-time enforcer who rose fast, mainly by killing his competition, and later branched off into his own thing. Not as a drug kingpin, although he had some dealings in pills and powder, unavoidable given his line of work. No, Crow made his mark off running girls and gambling dens of sin. He saw those businesses as a safer way to go. Crow knew he could still make a good living, a very good living, running poker and blackjack tables around the city and providing perks for the players without the ugliness that can come from the drug trade. The perks for the players were girls and the aforementioned pills and powder. He probably could have done all this without a ton of legal issues if it weren't for his unfortunate habit.

Crow enjoys killing people.

Women in particular.

Namely, the women he employs.

Remo feels a wave of nausea pass over him as he calculates the number of times he was able to successfully help Crow out of trouble. The number of women who died, killed by Crow, and how Remo made any form of justice for those crimes disappear. This is what Remo was trying to work out in his damaged brain before all this Cormack shit came into play. This is exactly the type of shit that pushed him to do what he did with the Mashburns.

Remo's guilt, the heaviness of it.

That's it, thinks Remo, that's really what this is all about. That's what set this whole damn shitshow in motion. Remo's guilt is what is powering all of this and he's got tons of it. He turns his head and watches as Lester disposes of Dutch Mashburn's head. Remo's own head fumbles around the truth.

The idea that his choice of profession has set him on this path. Perhaps sending him on a path that now has him standing in Central Park watching Lester jam a former client's head into a trash can. Perhaps this was something destined to be. Remo's not a deeply religious person, he'll leave all that shit to Lester, but Remo's thinking is skimming around the edges of predestination and the like.

Is this why Remo is here?

I'd like you to remove him from circulation.

That's what Cormack said.

Is Remo the instrument to undo the wrongs?

"There," Lester says, arm covered to the shoulder in the New York filth. "Bastard's skull is way down in there."

Hollis rolls his eyes.

Remo smiles and looks over Hollis and Lester. They can do this, he thinks. They can remove Crow from circulation and get clear of Cormack. Remo can be rid of the guilt he's been dragging around because of the Mashburns and Crow. There are many others Remo has helped get away with horrible things, but he's convinced his guilt will subside once Crow is done. The Mashburns and Crow will equal two wrongs undone. Two wrongs make a right, or some shit like that.

"What's our move?" asks Hollis.

Remo continues to smile and stare at them while his mind works it all the way through. Maybe he can write a tell-all book or hit the lecture circuit or teach or whatever. Find a new way to make a living once this is all over. He snickers to himself as he runs over the possibilities of a life post-guilt.

Lester and Hollis look to one another. *Remo's gone bye-bye.*

Remo can find a better way to make a living and maybe, just maybe, he can have a life with Sean. Anna will never come around, that ship has sailed. She has an immeasurable amount of hate for Remo that cannot be overcome. He realizes that and has made peace with it, but Sean? Maybe there can be more. Before all of this went down, all Remo wanted was to meet his son. It's what got him through the ordeal with the Mashburns. Hell, it's what made Remo start the ordeal with the Mashburns.

Now?

Now that he's met Sean, Remo wants more.

"Asshole?" Hollis says.

If taking down Crow will give him that chance, a chance with Sean, a chance to be some form of a father, then Crow needs to be removed.

Remo eyes Hollis and Lester.

Lester blinks, scraping some NYC goo from his arm.

Hollis raises his hands. "Well? What the fuck?"

"We're going to remove Mr. Crow from circulation and get our lives back."

Lester loves this idea. The excitement in his eyes is undeniable. There's an almost visible electric bounce ricocheting inside of him.

Hollis's assessment leans more to the unsure side of things. He knows Remo and knows no matter what Remo is saying, or the reasons he's saying it, there will be blood. Lots of blood. More than likely some of it will be Hollis's.

"You got a plan?" asks Hollis.

"No."

"The Lord has a plan," Lester says, showing his Bible.

Hollis shakes his head.

Remo grins. *Classic Lester.* "I think you're right, Lester."

"Okay." Hollis takes a deep breath. "How does the good Lord want us to remove Mr. Crow?"

"Don't be a dick," says Lester.

"It's a valid fucking question," Hollis says.

"I understand, but there's a certain tone you're using and I don't like it."

"Tone? Fuck my tone."

"See. That. That right there. That's the tone and it's offensive."

"You just shoved a man's head into a trash can."

"So?"

Remo steps in. "Gentlemen, we have to find a way to work together on this thing of ours. All three of us have to get this done. I can't do it alone and you both have your own reasons for doing this. We can all get clear and get where we want to go, but only if we don't tear each other apart."

Hollis and Lester glance at one another, but only a glance. They know Remo's right.

Lester extends his hand to Hollis.

Hollis looks at his filthy, head-dumping paw. "Not a chance in hell, but I accept what you're trying to do with that there."

"Gotta give me something," Lester says.

Hollis thinks, then gives him a half-hearted military-style salute.

Lester's eyes slip to Remo. *Really?*

Remo nods and salutes him as well.

Lester sighs and returns the gesture.

18

"We need to pull our money together," Remo says.

"Fuck you," says Hollis.

"Don't have any money. Not my thing. Material needs are for shit," Lester says, watching the lights blink and ding as the elevator climbs.

Remo realizes he jumped the conversation a bit. In his mind, they had already all agreed to team up in an alliance and go after Crow and end this thing. Meaning that they had all agreed to what needed to be done. Meaning that shit costs money and Remo ain't picking up the tab on all that shit.

He'll take the hit on this hotel room, that was his decision, Remo gets that, but everything else is going to cost. They'll need guns, for starters. They'll also need transportation, be it cabs, airfare or whatever. They might want to eat somewhere along the way. Might have to grease some palms for information. There's a lot of shit, man.

Remo opens his mouth, about to explain.

Hollis sticks a wad of cash into Remo's chest.

Remo catches it before it hits the floor. With a quick count it looks to be maybe a couple a hundred and change. Remo appreciates the gesture, but knows that isn't going to get this crew very far. That combined with what Remo has might get them through Crow, but after that, who knows.

There's no *going away* money.

No *starting over* money.

No *fuck you* money.

It may not seem like it, but a guy like Remo plays life like a game of chess. Thinking several moves ahead. Now, just because he's thinking of moves ahead of time does not mean the moves he's thinking of making are the best or the safest. The moves are almost never cloaked in morality—God knows that's not the case—but nonetheless he's always thinking ahead, and what he's thinking now is…

"We'll have to rob Crow too."

Ding.

The doors open to their hotel floor.

Remo steps out, leaving Lester and Hollis with his words hanging in the elevator like an unspeakable fart.

19

Remo heads straight to the bar in their hotel suite.

Lester and Hollis take a seat on the couch. The room has been cleaned and looks great. This is why Remo wanted a nice room to call their command center, and now that the issue of Dutch's severed head has been resolved they can sit down and figure this the hell out in a civilized manner.

"You want to explain?" asks Hollis.

Remo drops the cash Hollis gave him onto the glass table then begins pulling the cash from his pants and suit jacket pockets, letting the bills fall to the table. It's a fair amount of money. You'd be happy to win that pile in Vegas. But it's not all that impressive if you go big-picture and Remo knows it.

"That's it," Remo says, takes a gulp of Blue. "That's all we've got to go to war with Crow. My credit cards will be frozen any second now, and soon as they are they'll toss our asses the fuck out of this room."

"We should order some food," says Lester with a childish giggle.

Remo snaps his fingers and points to Lester. *Good idea.*

Lester finds the black leather menu by a glass lamp and begins to look it over.

"Order a shitload," Hollis adds. "A last-supper-style thing and some shit we can pack up and take with us."

Remo points to Hollis. *Now we're thinking.*

"So what are you thinking with Crow?" asks Hollis.

Remo pulls a laptop from his brown bag, along with the hard drive. While powering up, he plugs in the drive, letting everything boot and buzz. Remo takes another swig of Blue, letting the burn work its way down. Hollis gestures to pass the glass over. Remo thumbs toward the bar. *Get your own.* Hollis snatches the glass from his hand and drains it.

"Dick." Remo gets up and heads back to the bar, pours himself another. "Crow runs some big-money, exclusive poker games around Midtown." He brings the bottle over to the couch and refills the glass Hollis stole. "Lots of cash at these things. What I'm thinking, to answer your question, is take down one of those and pick up some folding money and maybe get some info."

"Maybe use it to set something else up," Hollis adds.

"What do you mean?"

Lester picks up the phone and begins ordering up the food.

Hollis continues. "I mean maybe we make it the beginning of a bigger plan. Maybe we hit a game and make it look like someone else did it. Flush out Crow. Get him on his heels, then smoke his ass."

Remo thinks on that.

It's raw, this plan, but it's forming. He likes it. He clinks his glass with Hollis. The laptop is booted up and running. Remo begins opening files and sorting through docs, scanned info and images. He turns the screen, allowing Hollis get a good look.

"Yes, that'll be all. Thank you," Lester says, hanging up and standing. "I'm going to take a shit."

"I'll alert the media," Remo says.

Lester heads down the hall to the bathroom.

Remo points to the screen. "That one. That game's been rolling strong for years. His biggest one."

"Pick a different one."

"Why?"

"Don't want to go big first time out. We want to get his attention, not declare war. We save the big one."

"Okay, I'm going to value your opinion on this here, but we might not get a choice on what we hit."

"Value. Yes, that's the right word. You 'value' my opinion."

"Don't have to be a dick about it."

"Oh, but I do."

There's a knock at the door. A woman's voice calls out from behind the door. "Room service."

Remo looks to Hollis. *That was quick.*

Hollis pulls his gun and rushes to check the peephole. A young woman dressed in hotel garb stands outside with a cart. Hollis nods to Remo but takes a place by the door with his gun at the ready. Remo flips the bolt and opens the door.

"Anywhere?" the woman asks, strolling in, pushing a cart that holds a silver dome.

"Over there by the couch is good," says Remo.

Hollis watches her. There's something off, but he can't place it. She doesn't move like a luxury hotel employee. Her walk. It's almost arrogant. Ballsy. There's a look to her too. It's unpolished. Her eyes are wild. Everything about her screams *proceed with caution*.

Hollis re-grips his gun, never taking his eyes off of her.

The woman follows Remo's request and leaves the cart next to the couch. With a wink and smile she exits, quietly shutting the door behind her.

Hollis checks the peephole. "Something's not right."

"What?" asks Remo.

Hollis moves over to the cart.

Lester comes back from the bathroom. "Grub's here?"

Hollis removes the silver dome.

Dutch's head rests on a silver platter.

20

"Well, that's just fucking fantastic," Remo says.

"Not what I ordered," Lester says, placing the dome back.

Hollis stares. Blinking. Thinking.

Remo starts pacing. His anxiety can be measurable by the speed of his speech and the wild, frantic motion of his hands. "What in the fuck is that doing back here? Is it some kind of message from some kind of motherfucking asshole? One of those sleep-with-the-fishes mafia motherfucking messages that requires de-fucking-coding. Huh? Anybody got an answer on this one?"

"Remo—" Lester says.

"What's the message sent when someone delivers the head of a dude that you just shoved in a trash can less than an hour ago? Love to hear it. Maybe someone thought we lost it and wanted to return it. Wonderful. Humanity lives."

Lester thinks of saying something, but stops himself.

Remo continues to work the carpet.

Hollis thinks, says, "Let's do the math. Your CIA boy maybe? Wants us to know he's got eyes on us?" He looks to Remo. No answer, only a blank stare. "Remo," Hollis snaps.

Remo stops his pacing long enough to suck down some Johnnie Blue. "Sorry, needed to drink."

"You've had your drink. Now, would Cormack do this?"

Remo ponders. "I don't know who else would."

"I don't either." Hollis turns to Lester. "You got any thoughts on the subject?"

"None other than, 'I'm still hungry.' I'm also annoyed we have to dump Dutch's head again. So, yeah, the combination of those is causing me to get upset. That's what I know."

Hollis can't help but bust a snort-laugh.

Remo follows with a childlike giggle.

Lester doesn't think it's funny. At all. As he's clearly stated, he's annoyed and hungry.

Remo and Hollis are now in a full-on roaring laughing fit. Hollis holds on to the wall for support while Remo falls on the couch. It's the absolute ridiculousness of their situation that's got ahold of them. The acceptance of being completely fucked has washed over them and all they have left to do is laugh. This acceptance hasn't reached Lester. "Why are you laughing?"

Remo barely gets out, "It's better than crying."

Hollis snorts. "We're so fucked."

"I know," Remo roars.

Lester snickers. The sound of others laughing is infectious. He begins to break up, as much as a man like Lester can. He leans forward, looking at the cart. There's a small wadded up napkin. Lester can make out the colors of a fast-food logo. His eyes go wide for a split-second. He gets control of himself, making sure the other two didn't see him. He carefully removes the napkin.

Hollis and Remo continue with the giggle fest.

Lester opens the napkin. "Shit."

"What?" asks Remo.

Lester quickly shoves the napkin deep into his pocket, then lifts the dome from over Dutch Mashburn's head.

"What are you doing?" Remo asks.

Lester picks up the head by the hair and jams it back into his rolling suitcase. "We can't leave it here."

"So we're going to keep it like a good luck charm?"

"Did I miss the good luck?" Hollis asks, wiping a tear from his eye.

A knock at the door.

Hollis pulls his gun. Lester pulls out the butcher knife from the suitcase.

Remo checks the peephole, pauses, then turns to Lester. "How much damn food did you order, man?"

21

Mr. Crow lives life like a Bond villain.

He enjoys dressing in the finest of clothes at all times. He carries a deep belief that the clothes do indeed make the man. At the moment, the clothes making Crow a man come in the form of a Kiton navy blue tuxedo. His dark hair is perfect, not a single one out of place. His appearance is a constant state of groomed.

His steady state?

Perfection.

His profession?

A career criminal of means.

Crow makes his daily bread off the weakness of others, no matter the sin. He's used all seven of those deadlies to pad his accounts, but the two main sins Crow's businesses focus on are greed and lust. He's found these to be the easiest to profit from. The simplest of mouse traps to build, but only if you know how to work the buttons right.

He's managed over the years to boil it all down into a profit center that scratches people's itches in a very efficient and profitable manner. If you go to a Crow establishment you know what you'll get. First you have to be invited, but if you do get the invite you'll get a world-class experience consisting of high-class gambling and girls. He added men to the mix a couple of years ago. The rise in the net worth of women and gay men in the city wasn't lost on Crow, and if you're going to grow your business you need to pivot with the times. He's reluctant to add trannies to the mix, but if there's a transgender whale who wants to pay to play, Crow will consider anything.

Crow's big problem?

It's a problem Remo has helped him with from time to time.

Crow enjoys killing.

Women in particular.

The working ladies of his parties to be even more specific.

Matter of fact, he's just killed one now.

There's a few drops of her blood sprayed upon his fine navy blue tux and across his face. Crow stands over her body as a neon sign blinks purple behind him. Even during the day it creates a brightly colored pulse to the otherwise depressing room of hers.

Crow holds a blood-soaked ballpoint pen in one hand.

His phone in the other, poised to call someone for some assistance.

He pauses, letting his eyes scan over his work. Allows his drumming heartbeat to wind down to a normal resting rate. The young blonde's mouth is still open, shock frozen on her face. Eyes wide open, looking for answers. For logic. For hope.

There will be none for her.

Those things ended a week and a half ago when she first met Crow.

She just didn't know it then.

She does now.

Crow leans down to the blonde, plays with her hair a bit, then softly says, "I'm going to find someone to come in here and take care of your mess." He wipes his face with a handkerchief, smearing the blood even more across his face. He locates a dirty mirror in the tiny bathroom. "I am sorry. It's sad you had to pull it out of me, but you did, didn't you?" He moves back into the room, standing over her. "You said the shit you said and now look at you. You had to go and make it this way. Didn't you, darling?"

Blood pumps from her neck.

Crow moves his foot to avoid it getting on his shoes.

"Gotta run now." Crow sighs big. "Sorry you fucked up."

His phone buzzes. "Yeah." Listens, then, "Okay. Table's good? Right? Good. Send a car." He almost hangs up but stops. "Hey, send some fresh clothes. Another Kiton. Black, pink tie."

Stepping over her body, he drops the pen on her stomach before walking out the door.

Crow walks down the hall with a slight strut in his step. He heads down the barely-lit hallway, passing a man laid out by a door sleeping one off, a stray cat licking his face. Noises from the walls thump and pound. Roars of arguments, of way-too-loud TVs and the muted sounds of abuse in its various forms.

Crow taps his phone, then scrolls down to a name.

A contact.

REMO.

22

Remo, Lester and Hollis are sprawled out in the hotel room.

Looks like they just took down a combination of Thanksgiving and a chili cook-off, and when they finished with that they requested a Vegas brunch buffet to top it off. Lester is laid out on the couch with his pants button popped open. Hollis can't breathe. Remo can only stare out the window from his position lying down on the couch. He'd suck his thumb if was alone. No one has said a word for at least fifteen, maybe twenty, minutes, which is some form of record with Remo.

Dirty plates and bowls litter the luxury room, along with food-caked utensils scattered around various tables and such. There's a soup spoon on the floor, buffalo wing stuck to the window and half a cake in the bathtub. Remo saw it when he took a piss. Didn't think to question it, but he did grab a piece with his free hand.

Remo's phone buzzes a few feet from him on the floor.

"Guh," Remo grunts.

The phone isn't that far away, but it's far enough to require some effort, and that's effort Remo would rather not expend at the moment.

Buzzes more.

"Get it, dammit," says Hollis. "It's pissing me off."

Remo pushes himself off the couch as if he was rising from a hospital bed after a long coma. Without looking at the screen he grabs the phone and slides his stuffed body down to the floor.

"Who is it?" Hollis asks.

Lester snores.

Remo cracks open one eye, making out the C, then the R. Both eyes fly open. Now they are completely wide and they can't believe what the hell they are seeing.

"It's fucking Crow," he says.

Lester stirs awake. "Answer it."

"Yeah, what the hell? Take the damn call," Hollis says.

Remo sucks in some air.

Closes his eyes tight.

Taps, then says, "Hello."

"Remo," Crow says. Remo hears a car door close. The engine fires up. "Need a little something from you."

"Crow?"

"Don't start, Remo. Don't start with your shit because I don't give a shit. What I do give a shit about is finding someone to assist me with a matter of mine. A matter that you can and will handle for me. A matter that I pay a rather large retainer to be handled by you and the pricks you work for."

Remo's mind goes nuclear. A mushroom cloud plumes inside his skull. He remembers the Crow cases. He's been so consumed with his own shit that he's almost forgotten who and what Crow is. Off the tone in his voice, the way Crow's talking, Remo knows what has happened. He's killed another one. Crow, probably minutes ago, ended the life of another woman. Heat rushes to Remo's face as if someone cranked the room up to a hundred. He feels his hands shake.

Hollis looks to Lester. Something's up with Remo. It's all over him. This is something they haven't seen out of Remo and they're not sure they like it. Remo is on the floor with his eyes closed. If they didn't know better, they'd think he was praying.

"You still there, Remo? I need. I need, man. I need your help, again," Crow says.

Remo tries to count the number of times he's had this conversation with Crow. The number of times they've talked like this, because that would equal the number of women Crow's killed. And if you're keeping score at home, that would also equal the number of times Remo has helped Crow get away with it.

Is it double digits?

"Remo?"

It can't be in the teens, can it? Bet it fucking is. This human garbage has killed so many he can't count them all. Can't count how many times he's helped this bucket of shit walk away free from murder.

"Remo, take an address. Fix this shit."

Hollis and Lester stand up, their eyes dead on Remo. They don't know what to do. The man they seek is on the phone. A strange, and possibly fortunate, twist of fate, and Remo seems to be melting down. If there's one thing these two know about Remo it's that Remo doesn't drop the ball. Remo is never sick at sea.

Hollis snaps his fingers. Not even sure why he did it.

Remo's head makes a quick jerk in his direction. They lock eyes.

Remo looks to Lester, who's gripping his prized Bible. Lester's gaze does not waver. Does not break. He does not blink or look away. His face is stone. It is as if he's saying everything, while offering up nothing. Remo isn't let off the hook with an encouraging nod or a look of sympathy. Not from Lester at least. Lester wants Remo to get there by himself. Wants Remo to make the right decision on his own. And if Remo doesn't, Lester might kill him.

Crow says, "Listen, motherfucker. You'd better get on this shit directly."

Remo looks to his new partners in crime and echoes the words he said to Crow about a week ago. "I can ease your troubled mind and heal your heavy heart."

"Fuck you, Remo. I'll meet you at your office in one hour," Crow says.

"No. Not there," Remo spits out in a panic. "I'll text a new place."

"Why?"

"The office is not a good place to talk."

"Again I'll ask you, *why?*"

"There's been some leaks. I don't trust it. Most of us are taking meetings off campus until things get patched up."

There's a pause on Crow's side of the conversation. Lester and Hollis share a look. Remo grips the phone tighter, rocking back and forth on the floor. If Crow goes to the office they are fucked and this opportunity will go away with the wind.

"Okay. Whatever. Meet me at my Hell's Kitchen place in an hour. Nobody's leaking shit there."

"Much appreciated." Remo half-smiles to Lester and Hollis as he lays down the phone. "I think we've got something."

Part III

He will die as he lived.

23

Remo, Hollis and Lester push out through the revolving doors of the Essex House, storming their way down West 59th.

Moving with purpose, like men on a mission. They wrapped up a discussion with a vague outline of a plan only moments ago. One that includes Remo taking advantage of this meeting. This sit-down.

This takedown.

They agree they might not get another shot at this. All that talk about which place to take down first and the money they'd get is over. Things change quickly in this life, so they need to be happy with whatever money they can get, if any, as long as they get their man. The main goal, meaning the goal of saving their asses, is to get to Crow. Of course, Lester isn't really in as deep as the other two. Remo lied to him a second ago, telling him that if Cormack had the head sent over, then he was on to Lester as well. *Lie* is strong word. Remo figures it's very possible, so in Remo's mind that's as good as the truth, not to mention Lester is a killing machine on a mission from God. That fact can come in handy if played correctly, and Remo is considered the motherfucking Jimmy Page of playing criminals.

"We'll need shotguns," Hollis says.

Lester nods, pulling the suitcase behind him.

"Need, or want?" asks Remo.

"Need, without question. Well, depends on the setup of the room."

"I've never been to this place."

"Based on the other places you showed me on that hard drive? Shotguns."

Remo doesn't know what they need. Only thing he knows is that they need Crow to go away and they were handed a gift by him calling. He also knows they need to get on with this thing before whoever dropped off that head decides to escalate things.

"Whatever. I don't care about the hardware, I just want to know if we can do this," Remo says.

After Remo hung up with Crow, Hollis explained that he's got a guy not too far from Crow's Hell's Kitchen money game who can hook them up with some tools, but it'll cost them. They worked out the finances. It's not great, but they can get armed to an acceptable level. That's not the problem. The bitch is they need to stop and get a change of clothes if they're going to have a chance of doing this thing right.

According to Remo's files, Crow's setup isn't the kind of thing you can just storm into with guns blazing. Oh no, no, no. Crow's a psychopath and royal motherfucker, but not an idiot. There are check points, access points and space between the entrance and where the party is. Meaning where Crow will be and, not to mention, where the money is.

Also, Crow is expecting his high-priced, attack-dog fixer of an attorney to show up. Not a hobo offering up five-dollar hand jobs plus gratuity. Remo needs to look the part. He needs to look like the guy Crow knows and hates, but needs dearly. Remo's suit is a wreck and Lester's (Remo's to be accurate) needs some freshening up. It's unclear when all of them will go in or how, so it's necessary for all of them to look like they belong at one of Crow's parties. So, logic suggests they need to spend some coin to fit in with the Midtown whales.

Remo luckily has a tailor not far from here. He works out of a shop at The Plaza, but he's not cheap, and considering this is going to be an extreme rush job the odds are this will be the biggest bill Remo's ever seen out of Mario the tailor. All of this is to say that once they get their shit together they aren't going to have much cash left. Not to mention that Remo's credit cards might get frozen any second, and they might not have a hotel room to come back to either.

So this thing, this Crow party takedown, better fucking work, because there's a good chance they will be penniless and homeless once it's over. Regardless of Cormack's agenda, they know they need to pick up a few dollars with this deal. Appeasing their new master in the CIA is still priority one, but what good is your freedom if you're just going to die the streets with no money? Remo's no animal. He's a man of comfort, and by God he's going to get those comforts back no matter the risks. Crow's party is a big first step. A step toward being free, clear and finding some scratch to build a life off of. Remo keeps thinking of Sean. One step at a time. If he can do this, maybe he can pull together a normal life and be some form of father to his son. It's possible. Maybe.

He has to live through his meeting with Crow first, of course.

That much is understood.

Remo stuffed as many of the to-go containers from room service as he could into his brown leather bag. It's flung over his shoulder and stinks of cheese and pork, but it's full of the stuff that's going to keep them alive. Food and evidence. Well, it *was* evidence. Now it's research. There was more room in Lester's suitcase, but Remo didn't want to put any of the food in that rolling disaster. The food's all closed up in the containers, but the idea of having your food anywhere near a severed head is a little gross. Even for this crew.

Time is short.

Divide and conquer.

Remo and Lester cross the street, heading toward The Plaza for some fine-ass threads. Hollis hangs a right, heading off to find his people and some proper instruments of mayhem.

"Shotguns, motherfuckers," Hollis mutters as he walks away, disappearing as if swallowed whole by the walking masses of New York.

24

The suit fits like a dream.

Remo immediately feels like a new man. Actually, the fine threads make him feel like his old self. It's a warm tingle of a feeling, like he was slipping back into character. The second Mario slid the jacket on it was as if a switch flipped and Remo the Wealthy-as-Hell Defender of Assholes was back online. Back in the game and reporting for duty.

He runs his fingers along the sleeves. Feels good. Nice. Feels right. Gray pinstripes with a purple tie and a classic stark, crisp white shirt. His black shoes shine like fucking mirrors. Remo never knew it, but the clothes actually do make the man.

Lester could give two shits.

He likes his suit. It's fine, or least that's what he told Remo, but his character didn't change. At all. The threads feel nice and all, but his focus is the same as it was a few minutes ago. Killing some folks to help out Remo and maybe himself, if Lester allowed himself to think about himself. The self-love thing is not exactly Christlike as far as Lester sees it, but he acknowledges the limitations God placed on people, so he deals with it best he can.

It comes and goes. Selfless to selfish. It's a struggle for every man, he knows, but he tries hard to suppress that shit. In regard to the suit, Lester is more concerned with things like: how easy is it to get his gun out and put a bullet in a motherfucker? What's it going to be like, running in this monkey outfit? There are some other hot-button topics on Lester's mind, like punching, kicking, gouging and stabbing, but gunplay is numero uno.

Remo catches Lester practicing violence in his new suit while looking in the full-length mirror. They got Hollis an off-the-rack job based on the size he gave Remo. Hopefully it fits. Remo guesses it doesn't really matter, but there's this part of him that hopes Hollis likes it. The way you give a buddy a gift and want them to show some appreciation for the thought. Remo has already played the scene out in his head. *Just shine it on and act like you like it, Hollis. For fuck's sake.*

Remo adjusts his tie in the mirror next to Lester, who's practicing strangling an invisible man. He's really getting into it, too. Lester's face is red. Veins in his neck are plumping up. Mario watches while attempting not to show on his face that his brain is screaming out *what the fuck?*

"We'll take 'em, Mario. All three," Remo says.

"Of course. I'll have them cleaned for you," Mario says, rushing to his side.

"No need, Mario." Remo hands him a stack of cash. "We'll be wearing them out."

Mario is confused. *This isn't the fucking Gap, man.*

Lester snatches up a fistful of candy from a crystal dish. "These free?"

Mario nods.

Remo feels an unexpected wave of emotion rush over him as he looks to Mario. "We've known each other a long time."

Mario nods.

It hits Remo.

Just now.

Surprising it wasn't until now that Remo thought of this.

He realizes he hasn't had time to think, but still, he should have had a slightly better handle on this situation. He hasn't been able to let his mind take a beat and think things through. Life has been a little hectic today. There's that, the constant pills and booze, but regardless, Remo should have at least thought about this before now.

Looking at Mario's round face, Remo has realized he may never be here again. He may never go anywhere he used to go only days ago. His old life is quite possibly gone forever. It's not just Mario, although he's very fond of the man. It's all of it. The whole thing. His whole life in New York. Where he lives. The routine of his life and the life he's lived being the biggest, baddest defense attorney in New York is quite possibly over. It was a damn fine routine.

Was being the correct word.

Tears begin to form in the corners of Remo's eyes. He places a hand on Mario's shoulder and squeezes. Perhaps a little too hard.

Mario is even more confused now than ever.

Lester practices stomping the invisible man's head.

Remo's life is in the process of changing forever, and for the first time in a long time he has no clue what's up next for him. No idea what the universe has up its sleeve. His former life was insane, no doubt, but there was a rhythm to it. A steady beat to the crazy. If you took a step back and looked at it in its entirety it all made some form of sense. At least it did to Remo. There was a sequence to life he could count on. Money, booze, pills, sex, self-loathing—these were the things Remo could rely on day in and day out.

Now?

He's got nothing.

Nada. Zip. He has no idea how he's going to earn a living, let alone how he's going to live. Where the next bottle of pills is going to come from. When he is going to get laid next. This new moment of clarity is almost as sharp and penetrating as the one that hit him when he first decided he should double-cross the Mashburns. It was so clear then. Simple. So easy. It was the right thing to do and Remo knew it. He didn't fight it. Little did Remo know when he made that quick, snap decision he was pushing reset on his entire life. The good and the bad.

"I'm sorry," Remo says, moist eyes looking deep into the shit-brown of Mario's. Mario gives a nervous smile, wishing he was anywhere but here.

Lester has the invisible man in a headlock.

Remo puts both hands on Mario's shoulders as the tears stream down his face. "I've got to go now. Thank you for everything."

Mario hands him a receipt.

25

The three men cut through the crowded streets like candidate for masters of the universe.

They are not tough-talking MBA pussies working a Wall Street desk.

Not at all.

These men are pissed and they are here to end someone's time on this planet.

They are here to kill a man named Mr. Crow.

They have no idea what to really expect in there. Remo has never met Crow at his place before. Their meetings have always been in the safety of a conference room at Remo's firm. He's heard the stories from Crow and others about what goes on at these places. He's seen some pictures here and there, but being there in the flesh is a much different type of deal. Reality can be a bit more complex.

From the outside the place looks peaceful enough. It's just a metal door at the bottom of a nondescript building located on the edge of Hell's Kitchen. There's an Asian noodle joint. A hipster coffee place on the corner. The city moves and buzzes around here as it does everywhere else. Busy New Yorkers move past them as if they were three simple little stones in a river. Flowing around them. Most of them annoyed, as if Remo, Lester and Hollis were intentionally keeping them from something important.

Hollis hate-watches a hipster yapping on his phone through some headphones.

Lester hates New York. Makes him itchy.

Remo checks his watch.

It's time.

Remo wants to vomit violently.

"You'd think this kinda shit would get easier," he says.

"It doesn't." Hollis puts a hand on Remo's shoulder. "Don't fuck it up."

Hollis slips off in the other direction, putting some distance between him, Lester and Remo. Lester raises his Bible, placing it next to Remo's head. "This is why I came back. You know that, right?"

Remo shakes his head no.

"You remember when I sat down with you at the Chinese place?"

"Before you got shot to shit?"

"Yes."

"I recall, yes."

"The reason I came then is the same reason I'm back now. I'm here to save you. Physically mainly, because you keep dicking around with dangerous people, but you need spiritual saving as well. You've done the hard part, Remo. You made a decision to undo the evil you helped inject into the world. That's the path you chose. Like it or not."

"You coming, Jesus freak?" Hollis calls out from across the street.

Lester gives him the finger then turns back to Remo. "This is just the beginning."

"Beginning? Thinking it's lookin' more like the end."

Lester gets closer, locking eyes, about a half-inch from Remo's nose. "No, friend. This place you're standing? That door over there? Crow? This is the start of something. A revolutionary war that you started. We can wage it together."

Remo is now even more terrified.

Lester giggles like a child with an ice cream cone as he bounces off, leaving Remo and heading toward Hollis across the street.

Remo watches them walk farther and farther down the street. He knows they are taking their place. This was part of the half-assed plan they had. Them heading to their starting blocks for this little project that's about to go down at Crow's. Never in a million years did Remo think he would see those two people, his clients technically, together in the same place at the same time, let alone walking and talking together, involved in a plan, with Remo, to remove Crow, another client, from the earth at the request of the CIA.

It's a lot to stomach.

Much too much to take in.

Remo pops a pill, chasing it down with his flask of some Johnnie Blue.

He shuts his eyes, squeezing them tight. So tight he sees spots.

His big brain works his new world over. Turning it over and over and over again. Taking in all the angles of the situation and the endless possibilities of what he's about to do. Most of the possible outcomes he comes up with end with him being skinned alive and fed to stray cats. This is the spiral of bad things. If a person of Remo's intelligence is allowed to think for too long, then the darkness is going to eventually creep in. He shakes his head hard in an attempt to reset his head. Restart his thinking.

He thinks of Sean at the end of his hospital bed.

The smile on that kid's face.

Skinny elbows propping up his glowing face. The sound of his laugh.

Remo's eyes snap open.

He charges toward the door that'll lead him where he wants to go.

Hopefully to Sean and not down the path of getting Remo obliterated.

"Hug a nut, Crow."

26

The room is devoid of natural light.

Almost like a luxury bomb shelter.

The place probably had windows at one time, but they have been bricked over and painted long ago. Smooth jazz tickles the eardrums. There's a surprising hint of freshness to the air as well. The place actually smells like a four-star hotel. Remo is in a smaller room, a security post of sorts, that's off the main room. He can only make out parts of the larger room through a small square window located on a stainless steel door in front of him. Remo gets pushed through the metal detectors and patted down by several pairs of large, thick hands. He's fairly sure what's happening is bordering on sexual assault. A hand cups his nuts. A thumb grazes the cusp of his anus.

"Is this absolutely fucking necessary?" Remo asks Crow as his phone and wallet are removed from his pockets.

"Yup," Crow replies with a smirk. "Everybody goes through it. It's for everybody's safety and enjoyment." He looks Remo up and down. "New suit?"

"Yeah, got it today."

"Mario?"

"There anybody else?"

"No, there is not."

The wall of muscle shoves Remo forward, nodding to Crow that he's clean. Remo turns around and considers calling them cunts, but thinks better of it. This is not the time or the place for that kind of talk. Besides, these men are the size of grizzly bears and, also, if all goes well, Lester and Hollis will execute the lot of them soon enough.

"This way," Crow says, showing him toward the door that leads into the main room.

Remo steps through, holds his breath as he crosses the threshold.

It's a large dark room, lit just enough to see what you need to see. The jazz is only slightly louder as the waves of sound slide over the room, providing a mellow, chilled soundtrack to the place. It's like a high-end bar in a swank part of town. At the far end of the room is a towering monument of a bar made of sheets of glass and bottles of booze. It reaches from floor to ceiling. Has to be at least twenty-plus feet high. There are two bartenders on duty. One flips drinks around like a pro and the other is climbing a ladder to reach the good stuff up top.

Remo, a bit of an expert in gentlemen's clubs, quickly notices this place resembles some of the nicer titty joints he's visited over the years. Subtle differences, but there are some. There's no stage, no hip-hop cranked to brain-thumping levels, but there are young, attractive women slinking about the place dressed to seduce and titillate. One by one Remo watches them parade across the room, then take a seat in the laps of men. The women are all fully clothed, but Remo notices that in the short time he's been here, after some forced laughter and playful flicks of the hair, he's seen at least two women lead men into other rooms. Upon closer inspection, there are rooms located on the sides of this room. A row of what seems like smaller rooms on the right and left of where Remo and Crow are standing. An Asian beauty leads a potbellied fifty-something into one of the rooms a few feet to the right of Remo.

The men are a mix of old and new money. No telling how many are in the smaller rooms, but Remo counts ten sitting at the tables and booths of the main bar. He knew Crow ran some prostitution, but didn't know about this club in particular. Remo thought Crow's main vocational interest was gambling, but there is not a single poker or blackjack table anywhere he can see. There's also no sign of drugs. From afar it simply seems like a high-end whorehouse on the edge of Hell's Kitchen.

Crow kisses the hand of a tall brunette. She smiles.

Remo wants to tell her to run away as fast as she can.

"There somewhere we can talk?" he asks Crow.

Crow smiles to the brunette and waves her off. He shows Remo to a large, circular booth in the back corner. It's the only table where no one else is seated. Remo quickly surmises this must be Crow's understood office space. His floating work area.

"Drink?" Crow offers.

"Johnnie—"

"Blue, neat." A leggy redhead finishes his sentence, handing him a glass with a soul-melting smile. She slinks off before Remo can thank her.

"Nice place," Remo says, looking around, trying to

understand where the exits are. It's something he's become accustomed to doing when he walks into a room. He always wants to know how to get out. In his line of work, you never know what will happen in a room. As far as he can tell there's only the one way in and out, the way he came in originally, but he knows there has to be some way to get out in the back.

"This can't be it. More in the back?" Remo says, hoping Crow will help him with the layout.

"There's more," Crow says, sipping a vodka martini. "I'll give you a tour after we talk a bit."

"Sounds wonderful. Now, who did you kill this time?"

"Easy, friend-o. Need a little loving before you shove it in."

"Well, *friend-o*, that's why I'm fucking here, right? Or did you plan on taking me into one of those little side rooms for a tussle?"

Remo notices there's a female client being led by a chiseled, Latin model of a man. He's never seen a woman smile so big as she brings the bottle of Red along with her and slaps his ass with her free hand.

In the short amount of time Remo's sat there with Crow he's noticed the place has cleared out. There's nobody else sitting in the main room except for Crow and Remo. A goon of a man, also about the size of a bear, steps over to the table and whispers into Crow's ear. Crow nods, then waves him off.

"I need to have you clean up something for me," Crow says to Remo.

Remo tries not to be a dick but he can't take it. "What the fuck is wrong with you? I mean seriously."

"What?"

"Every damn time I talk to you you've killed some poor woman who trusted you. Why? Why do you need to do that, you fucked-up piece of shit?"

Remo realizes that might have come across a little strong.

Crow drinks his drink with a puzzled look on his face, looking as if his loyal dog has learned to talk.

"Tell me you've got a condition. Tell me it's something rare. Something way the fuck out there. Something so complicated, such a mental shitshow, that nobody can even vaguely diagnose the sewer you've got flowing between your ears."

Crow blinks, drinks, pulls out a pen and scribbles something on a scrap of paper.

"Is it as simple as you get off to it?" Remo asks. "That it? It's just about feeling sexy, sexy. Being a normal scumbag pimp isn't enough for you to get the juice flowing. You have to kill someone. Tell me that's not it. Tell me you're not a garden-variety TV bad guy. Say it ain't so, because that's just fucking sad, man."

Crow places a gun on the table, sips some more of his martini, and folds the scrap of paper into a neat little note.

"Done?" he asks, slips the folded note to Remo.

As Crow slides the note over to him, Remo wishes Hollis and Lester would hurry the fuck up. He knows the damn plan, knows they aren't coming in for another ten minutes, but he really wants to see Crow's brains blown out.

Soon.

Like now.

Remo has never liked Crow, even from day one he hated the prick, but now, after all he knows about him, he can't even bear

113

being in the same room with the guy. Disgusted to breathe the same air as Crow. Remo can't even find the strength to hide the contempt on his face as he opens Crow's note.

Scribbled across the paper are two simple words.

I KNOW.

27

Hollis and Lester stand in a nasty-ass alley.

Sporadic waves of people move past the two open ends of the alley, with the occasional pedestrian strolling through, looking to cut some time off their journey. At the moment, a homeless man is pushing a baby stroller filled with cans past them while murdering a Lady Gaga song at the top of his lungs.

Hollis checks the two sawed-off shotguns he's got stuffed into a green Nike bag along with some boxes of shells, then checks the Glock tucked inside his shoulder holster. Lester slides his Bible into his roller suitcase, then looks to his cracked Timex that's barely ticking. It's off by twenty-three minutes, but Lester knows this and makes the mental calculation each time he looks at it. Material things don't interest him, and the idea of shopping for a new watch doesn't really appeal to him either. He'd rather just work the math.

They look to one another, then look away.

Nothing to do now but wait and they know it.

The silence is deafening. Uncomfortable.

Damn uncomfortable.

This is a first for these two guys. The first time these two have been alone together and the conversation is not flowing.

Not at all.

Even though they have several things they need to discuss. Like, say, how they plan on doing this gun-blazing thing they are about to run face-first into. They've only thinly talked through the details, which is to say they've decided they are going to kill anyone who causes them a problem. Hollis is usually much more prepared—it's what he does, meticulous with the details of every job—but this time he has more or less resigned himself to a *grip it and rip it* philosophy. Hollis's recent personal and legal issues have caused him to relax his standards to a lower level than usual. Besides, he doesn't have much to go on anyway. Remo didn't know the layout. They assumed Crow's people would take his phone and check him when he went into the place. It was the protocol of all Crow's other establishments, so what the hell are they supposed to do?

Spend hours banging their heads against the wall? Waste a ton of time building a sound strategy?

No point.

Nope.

Tearing in with guns blazing was the best they had to go on. Rather than tell Remo that he had no idea what to do, Hollis made up some bullshit about waiting twenty minutes so Remo can get Crow and his people relaxed. Soften them up, make them comfortable. Hollis figured that line of crap beat the hell out of no plan at all. He also noticed Remo was becoming a bit fragile about this thing, so Hollis decided he really needed Remo to be Remo and not some quivering scoop of jelly. Still, as true as all this is, Hollis is uncomfortable about the wall of silence between him and his new partner, Lester. If you're going into a battle with someone, you'd like to think they care if you live or die. At the minimum.

"You like TV?" Hollis asks Lester.

"I like it, don't watch it."

"Oh, right, the religious thing?"

"No, I can separate entertainment from my faith. It's more that lately I've either been incarcerated or in a hospital or on the run from people trying to put me in the hospital, jail or the grave."

"Got it."

More creeping silence.

They check their watches.

Lester does the time-math and opens his mouth, about to say something, but thinks better of it. He wants to be better acquainted, too. They don't have to be best boys or anything, but he knows the value of working with a tight crew. He's seen a lot of jobs go shithouse when the men involved didn't trust or hated one another. Honor among thieves is rare, which is why he's known a lot of people in the joint who either lack honor themselves or got pig-fucked by some honorless asshole.

Deciding to bail on the *how's the family* small talk, Lester keeps his mouth shut. He remembers hearing Hollis saying something about how Remo has ruined all of that for him. Lester thinks it's probably best not to bring that shit up minutes before they're supposed to go storming in to save him.

"How long have you known Remo?" asks Lester.

"Too fucking—" Hollis pauses mid-sentence.

Something catches his eye.

A blur coming in fast, ripping down the alley hard as hell.

He pushes Lester clear at the last second. A 2x4 cracks Hollis in the face. The thick whack knocks him back, stumbling into a brick wall. Lester looks up in time to get the same weapon of wood slapped to his forehead followed by a hurricane-spin whack to the side of his head. The moves of this wood-wielding villain are like mini lightning strikes. Fast. Powerful. Relentless. Lester spins around helpless, tripping over his own feet, dumping himself into a swamp-like puddle in the middle of the nasty-ass alley.

Hollis pulls his shoulder Glock.

The end of the 2x4 jams hard into his ribs. Again and again, cracking his bones with rapid-fire speed. Air escapes his body in a flash. His teeth chomp down on his tongue as the 2x4 whips under his chin with mind-numbing force. Hollis falls back, bouncing off the bricks.

His sight blurs.

Head buzzes.

Through all of it, Hollis thinks that he might recognize their attacker.

He watches the alley warrior drop a wad of paper on Lester's busted-up face. Looks like a wadded up napkin. A fast-food napkin. Hollis realizes he's seen this person before. Recently as a matter of fact. He can't get his mouth to move or his body to react fast enough, but he's damn certain he knows this person. All he can do is watch the woman sprint away out the alley like a nimble, lost deer disappearing into the city. He staggers over to Lester. His eyes are shut, he's breathing, but not moving or responding to anything. Hollis shakes him hard, trying to get him to come around.

Hollis slaps him.

"Lester," he yells in his face.

Nothing. Lester is out like a light.

"Fuck," Hollis says, leaning back in the alley.

His mind floats back to the woman who beat their asses moments ago.

It's her.

It's the same woman from hotel room service.

The one who returned Dutch's head to them on a platter.

"What the fuck is her problem?"

28

I know.

I know is what Crow's little note said.

Troubling.

This could mean all kinds of shit.

Big question is: what exactly does Crow know?

Remo runs through the possibilities. Does Crow know about Hollis and Lester about to storm in blasting like the Wild Bunch? About Cormack? What exactly does this asshole know? There's only one way to find out, thinks Remo. Of course, he only has a split-second to form a question that'll keep him alive, but at the same time make everything seem like no matter what Crow knows, *that* knowledge is all bullshit and Remo is Crow's boy. Like he always was and always will be.

Remo decides to go with…

"Wow. I am over-fucking-whelmed. What in the fuck do you think you fucking know?"

Remo lets that float over the conversation.

Crow leans back, studying Remo. Eyes scanning him up and down. Remo can see his mind crank. There's some serious calculations going on in there. Crow licks his lips, then snaps his fingers. Two of his bear-sized goons step up, moving closer to the booth as casually as a lazy waiter. The smooth jazz still plays, but the place feels like it's suddenly gone deadly silent. Air in the room is now incredibly tight. Crow leans in close, allowing his stare to bore through Remo. He gently raps his fingers on the grip of his gun that waits patiently on the table. Remo feels his heart bounce up into his sinuses. Not knowing what's about to happen with a guy like Crow is not comforting.

"What went down in the Hamptons, Remo?" Crow finally asks.

"Why? What did you hear?"

"Things."

"Things like what? You heard I got into a shootout with some dissatisfied clients. Is that what you know so much about?"

"That, plus a little more."

Remo feels some relief. If all Crow knows about is the Mashburn showdown, he can wiggle out of that. Explain it away as a misunderstanding among irrational people. That'll work. Yeah. Maybe. The problem now is that *a little more* line of bullshit Crow added on the end there. Remo needs to know what else Crow is hanging on to. What else is drifting around in this psycho's skull.

"Well, don't play hard to get. Stick it in. What else ya got?" Remo asks.

Crow sips his drink. Raps his fingers on his gun.

Remo fights to keep his eyes from bugging out. *Where. The. Fuck. Are Lester and Hollis?* Remo wants to check his watch so bad he can taste it.

121

"You don't think that's enough?" Crow asks.

"It's a lot, to be sure, but I thought you found out I fucked your sister."

Crow cocks his head. Remo has decided to play this angle, regretting it a bit at the moment, but deciding it was all he really had. Jokes work most times.

This isn't one of them.

Crow looks like he swallowed a bug.

"I didn't fuck her," Remo says. "She's a lady. Only heavy petting, and by heavy petting I mean oral, and by oral I mean blowjobs, and by blowjobs I mean a lot of—"

Crow slams his palm down on the table. His gun and drink jump up off the wood. Remo saves his Johnnie before it dumps over. He chugs it down as if it was his last. Just might be.

"You know what else I know, Remo? I know you don't have a law firm anymore. I know you're not lawyer. Not anymore."

"Well shit."

"So if you're not a lawyer, and that seems to be the case, then the big question is what in the name of sweet fuck are you doing here?"

"Missed you?"

Crow looks to his bear-goons. They move toward Remo like he's a sugar-coated slab of meat as they put their paws on him.

"Oh come the fuck on, man. This isn't right. You and me got history. I came here for a business opportunity."

"Bullshit," says Crow.

"Okay fine. I've got nothing. I was going to tell you about all that unpleasant shit. I was. I need your help, man. I need help to get back on my feet."

Crow snaps his fingers.

The bear-goons pull Remo by the arms, dragging him out from the booth kicking and screaming. They yank him up upright and drop him on his feet facing Crow. Crow slides out from the booth, adjusts his suit, finishes the last drop of his martini. "I do have an opening. A business opportunity."

Remo does not like the look on his face, or his tone for that matter.

Not one bit.

"You a gambling man, Remo Cobb?"

29

Remo is dragged past the towering bar into the darkness.

Legs and arms flailing like a pissed off two-year-old.

The bear-goons manhandle Remo into the back of the place through a set of dark curtains. A light flicks on.

Remo gets shoved through the entrance of a six-inch thick metal door that resembles the entrance to a bank vault. The inside of this new room looks and feels a lot like a high-end poker room. All dark save for a few well-placed single bulbs that hang from the ceiling by black cords. There's another well-stocked bar along the far wall with some long, plush purple couches positioned around a stainless steel table that seats four. The couches and table are empty at the moment. The chairs at the table are pushed out, as if awaiting guests.

The smooth jazz that filled the other room is gone.

This room is quiet. A vacuum. As if shut off from the world.

Remo makes a note that two more bear-goons man both sides of the entrance. Their suit jackets bulge from their shoulder holsters. Once Crow enters the room the vault-like door is closed and locked by another bear-goon cranking a wheel.

Remo can feel his luck drain out from his ass as he watches the wheel turn. With each crank his hope gets smaller and smaller. The muscles in his face sag. He chews the inside of his cheek. Stomach twists in knots knowing there's no way in hell Lester and Hollis are busting through that thing. Hollis and Lester are good, but cracking a door like that and taking down Crow and his team of bear-goons is not damn likely.

"Any chance I can go to the bathroom?" Remo asks.

"None," Crow replies.

"Need to drop a deuce."

"Might not be a problem for long."

Remo doesn't have time to process Crow's statement. Out from the darkness step the men and women Remo saw earlier in the other room. The ones who went into the smaller rooms and the ones who showed them the way. Remo notices that all of them have a bit of a post-coitus glow about them as they pass under the lights. Some more than others. The pros seem to be shining it on with fake signs of how amazing it was.

Remo knows the look.

The men and women take their places on the purple couches that circle the lone table, creating an audience of sorts. They sit and wait. Their faces seem solemn in nature. Almost respectful, as if they were attending an event that required much respect. No one says a word. Eyes forward. Mouths shut. It's as if everyone knows what's up except for Remo.

Remo's heart pounds.

His breathing becomes minimal. Short, quick. In and out and only as needed. Teeth grinding while trying to control the fear spiking higher and higher with each passing second.

Crow watches Remo squirm. He loves it. He smiles, then nods to someone out of view. From the darkness steps a dapper man dressed in a classic tux with a red rose pinned in his lapel. His jet-black hair is slicked back and he looks like he lives at a gym and has an everlasting tan. Holding an envelope in one hand, he holds a leather box balanced on his fingertips with the other. Treating the box as a special thing. He presents the box to the crowd for a viewing.

Remo looks over the faces of the crowd seated on the couches. There's a mix of wide eyes, nods and an *ooooh* or two. A few members of the crowd clap. A couple of others whoop and laugh. This is what they've been waiting for. Whatever the hell this guy and his damn box are up to is what they came here to see. The side room sex was an extra. A bonus. Make no mistake that this, this thing here in this room with all the theatrics, is the main event these people came for. The Dapper Man sets the leather box down in the center of the table, directly under the light. Stepping back, he addresses the room like the master of ceremonies that he is.

"Welcome. We have a great evening planned for you. Have you enjoyed yourselves so far?"

The room breaks into applause. A few of the ladies in the room lay big kisses on their *dates*. They mess with their hair and give them loving, false as hell, but nonetheless warm looks. The woman client slaps her Latin boy toy and spits in his face.

"Well, I hope you have. That's what we do here. A full experience taking you from one end of the spectrum to the other. An experience of extremes in a short amount of time." He pauses. "You've enjoyed the rush of pleasure. Have you not?"

More from the crowd.

"Now comes the rush of risk." He pauses for dramatic effect. "A rush that can only come from taking a true risk. You all have money. Great success. Merely gambling money provides a bit of an uptick in heartbeats, right? But not like this." He points to a few in the group. "Some of you have been fortunate enough to be repeat guests. Congratulations, truly. That's impressive. Impressive that you're back, but more impressive that you wanted to do it again." He raises a drink. "Salute."

Remo watches the room in disbelief. *What the hell is happening here?*

The Dapper Man downs his drink and hands the empty glass to a bear-goon. He looks out over the group. Waits, then steps to the table. Remo finds it hard to find air, as if it's been sucked out of the room. There's an intensity that fills the area. It can be felt. In your stomach. On your skin. It's as if the scientific makeup of the room has actually changed. There's a clear moment where time has hit pause. Time has simply stopped as the room waits for the Dapper Man to reach the table. He places his hand on the box, then looks over the group.

"He's good. He's milking the moment," Crow whispers to Remo. "Watch."

The Dapper Man opens the box.

Remo wilts.

Crow laughs.

The group erupts with excitement.

The box holds a gun.

30

The chrome revolver shines under the light like a diamond in a goat's ass.

Sitting, resting in its velvet bed inside the box, the gun lies waiting for an outcome.

Remo can guess what that might be.

What outcome Crow has in mind.

The Dapper Man turns to Remo and offers him a chair. "We have a special guest. A first-timer who is eager to compete this evening."

"You could've let me get laid first," Remo says.

Crow shrugs. *Sorry.*

Remo looks to the bear-goons, who are seconds away from *placing* Remo in that chair. Accepting his limited options, Remo takes a seat at the table. The group cheers him on. A bartender sets another Johnnie Blue in front of him. At least Crow was good enough to give him that, thinks Remo. The Dapper Man calls up another two from the crowd. Two men. One in his sixties, a man made of old Manhattan wealth that seems to ooze from his pores. His suit is crafted in the finest of quality, but dated in style. He removes a cigar from inside his jacket and lays it on the table in front of him. The second man represents new money. Thirties, yoga-fit, with jeans that equal a Lexus payment.

Remo's eyes scan over the two of them. They carry very different exteriors, but both seem to have the same tangled ball of emotions underneath. There's a mix of fear, regret and a sense of *how the hell do I get out of this* trapped bouncing behind their eyes.

The Dapper Man removes the gun from the box and holds it above his head, presenting it to the room in a samurai-like fashion. The box is quickly removed from the table by the bartender. Everything is orchestrated. Every single one of Crow's staff seems to have a purpose, and they all have their timing down. Even the Dapper Man seems to be operating off a script. Remo's fairly sure he saw Crow's lips move while the Dapper Man delivered his "pleasure and extremes" speech. Remo can't help but wonder when they practiced all this. Is there a team meeting before they open? Are there training classes for new hires?

"You know the name of this game," the Dapper Man says.

The room explodes into roaring applause.

He removes a single golden bullet from his jacket. Again holding it up for the room to see. The light bounces off the shine of the polished tip. The crowd's applause grows even louder. The Dapper Man makes sure Remo sees it before he opens the cylinder. As he slips the bullet into the gun he says, "A lethal game of chance."

Two of the bear-goons walk through the room, making sure to stop at the guests seated on the couches, accepting their cash as if working the offering plates at a church. Another set of bear-goons make quick taps on iPads, taking notes as they accept the money. Remo can't believe it. They're taking bets. This shouldn't be a surprise to Remo, but it is. He truly can't believe this happening. That human beings are gambling on Russian roulette and, more to the point, that he's in the middle of it.

An aging millionaire seated on a couch across the table from Remo whispers into a young girl's ear. She nuzzles close to his cheek, whispers and points at Remo. He nods, then hands over a stack of cash, pointing his boney finger at Remo as well. He's putting his money on Remo per the young lady on his lap. Remo can't help but feel appreciative. Ya know, because they believe in him?

The young girl blows Remo a kiss.

Remo stares at her blankly. For a second he thinks about using his hand and tongue to act out a blowjob in response to her, but he lacks the conviction at the moment.

"All bets are in," says the Dapper Man. "No more bets." He waves his arm about the room and looks over the people seated at the table. The contestants of the game. Never allowing his world-class showmanship slip, not for a second, he raises the gun up over his head again.

He spins the chamber.

A hush falls over the room.

The group watches, on the edges of their seats.

Remo glances to his watch. It's past the time. Hollis and Lester should fucking be here by now.

Where the hell are they?

What the fuck, man?

They're not coming.

The Dapper Man slaps the cylinder in place. "Six chambers. One bullet. This gun is maintained and weighted perfectly, so there is precisely a one in six chance of a player drawing a loaded chamber."

He lays the gun down in the center of the table and stands to the side, looking to Crow. Waiting for the signal to start the game.

Remo turns to Crow, who still stands near the vault-like door, surrounded by bear-goons. Remo's thoughts slide, surprisingly, to his father. To how his old man died. Not exactly like this, but it was similar. The old man died in a shootout during a card game in Texas. He caught a hanger off his deal, revealing he was cheating like a bastard. The old man died facedown on the table after a couple of bullet blasts blew a hole in his chest the size of a pizza. It occurs to Remo he might very well bite it in a similar way. Different game. Poker versus Russian roulette. Bullet to the head versus the chest, but the result will be the same. Dead via gun. Facedown on a table. Remo thinks of his son and wonders if he'll have the same memory of his father. Will Sean ever know Remo died this way? Will Sean even know Remo is dead at all?

The Dapper Man waits for Crow.

Crow smiles big and nods at Remo, his new favorite player.

"Whichever player the barrel stops on starts us off tonight," the Dapper Man says, flipping the gun around with his finger.

The gun spins.

Round.

Round.

Round and…

31

Remo places the gun to his head.

His heart beats faster than a vibrator stuck on eleven. His fear is ratcheted up so high he doesn't even feel it, so damn intense it seems like it's not even present. There's a buzz that started in his stomach and has now taken over his entire body, a feeling Remo has never known before. He's been afraid before, sure, but this is a different brand of fucked up. Different from anything he's dealt with up until today. Different from any courtroom. Different from anything with the Mashburns. Way different. The thought of knowing you might kill yourself without wanting to kill yourself is a damn odd thing to get your mind around. However, Remo knows damn well that if he doesn't pull this trigger he's a dead man anyway. Crow will see to that for sure.

Remo turns toward Crow.

That smug fuck.

Standing there in his suit in complete control of this whole thing. The murderer who will continue to get away with it. At least he won't have Remo around to help him anymore. That is what passes for comfort at a moment like this. Remo's trembling hand holds the barrel of the gun to his temple.

Crow raises his drink, saluting Remo with a wink.

Remo makes a decision in that moment. In that moment he decides he's not going to give this dickhead the satisfaction of knowing his fear. Remo will not show him how damn terrified he truly is. No way he'll let Crow think he's won. Nope. If Remo is to die right here, tonight, then he will go out on his own terms and in his own way.

He will die as he's lived.

Like a complete asshole.

Remo downs his Blue then throws the glass directly at Crow's head.

Crow drops down as the glass barely sails over his skull, shattering on impact with the vault door. Shards of glass fall, bouncing off the floor. There are a few gasps, along with open mouths, across the room. Crow whips his head back around to Remo, who's shooting him the finger with his free hand, gun still held to his head with the other.

Remo looks Crow dead in the eye and pulls the trigger.

Click.

Half the crowd goes wild. The other half is pissed.

Count Crow as one of the pissed.

"Somebody bring me a bottle." Remo slams down the gun. "I can do this all night, motherfuckers."

32

Another dead millionaire gets dragged away with half a head missing.

That makes six now.

The bear-goons move quickly to clear the remains as fast as they can. Remo drinks directly from the bottle now. He's been at this awhile, and is getting pretty lit at this point. The last time around he stuck the barrel up his nose and pulled the trigger.

Remo thinks this must be what it's like when Jordan or LeBron slip into a zone. When no matter what kind of shot they throw up it goes in, hitting nothing but net. The hoop becomes the size of a swimming pool. They simply cannot miss. Only difference here is Remo doesn't want to shoot and certainly doesn't want to hit anything. He gets that, but the principle is the same.

Crow burns by the door.

Face red.

Fists and teeth clinched tight.

With every click Remo draws from the gun Crow can feel himself dying inside. That, along with the fact Remo is now singing Toto's "Africa" at the top of his lungs. Despite all of Crow's anger, the group is enjoying themselves. Money is changing hands and more and more people are putting their money on Remo. He's the people's champion, until he gets a loaded chamber at least.

Remo, now completely hammered, pauses his signing only long enough to do the fake blowjob thing toward the girl who originally whispered about betting on (or against) him. It's tasteless, to be sure, but even more so now, since the same guy she was sitting on a while ago is now being dragged off with half his head gone. Hers is not a sentimental business, but still, she'd rather not see the old guy killed in front of her.

The Dapper Man calls over two more players, who cautiously take their seats at the table next to Remo. They are much more nervous than the previous contestants. Egos gone. Bravado is a memory. Remo is on a heater of a streak and nobody in that room wants to go head to head with this guy.

One of them is the lone female player. Mid-forties and the owner of a successful clothing line. She started with nothing and clawed her way to the top, but the top can be boring once you get there. She gave up the drugs years ago and has nothing left to prove in business. She also got rid of her husband around the same time she gave up drugs and now focuses on herself, and brother, she gets bored easily. At the moment, however, she really wishes she'd picked another way to scratch that itch. Should have just paid to fuck the Latin kid rather than fuck with all this gun shit.

Remo senses her terror. She's not up for this. He knows they're all grownups here, but still, he feels a little sorry for her.

He's not sure if that's sexist or not. He didn't give two shits about the men who stepped up to the table, blew their heads off and got dragged away. Should he feel empathy for her and not for them? It's a troubling question for the drunk-as-fuck Remo Cobb. Whatever the social or political right and wrong of the thing is, Remo decides communication is the key.

"This looked more fun from the cheap seats, didn't it?" Remo asks her.

She nods.

"Want a drink?" He tries to hand her the bottle. "It helps a lot."

She waves it off.

The Dapper Man spins the gun. Her eyes bulge.

"You sure?" Remo asks, offering her the bottle again.

She takes it this time. The barrel points her way. She chugs. Remo watches her hands shake. A tear falls.

"Let her out," Remo says to Crow.

"What did you say?" Crow asks.

"Fine, fuck it, I'm a sexist dickhead, but she's not into this game. Not her thing. You've got her money. She's not going to talk, she can't; she's a witness to all of this and will go to jail. Let her out of her turn."

Under normal circumstances she'd be hostile as hell about Remo's obvious *big man* bullshit taking place here. All that *oh the little lady can't handle it* shit she's had climb her way over the years. But at this particular moment she's more than happy to let Remo be an asshole. She'll happily tap out of this game and play the poor, terrified vagina card.

About time it paid off.

"I'm not into this shit either," the other man at the table says, thumbing toward Remo. "Not against that one."

Crow watches the room. The rest of the people seem to agree. He sees the nods. The blank stares. The mood has shifted dramatically. The rest of them have finally put themselves in that seat and they want nothing to do with it. Nobody here wants to go up against Remo. Understandable. They've sat there and watched six people's heads explode while playing against him. They may not be a superstitious crowd, but after a while you start to believe it's just Remo's night.

Remo smiles big as shit at Crow.

A self-satisfied grin that comes from pissing all over someone's big plan.

Crow comes close to letting his rage get the best of him. He lets the hostility rise up, lets it cloud his thoughts, lets it muddy the waters. He thinks of grabbing a gun and blowing Remo's brains out himself, but doesn't. He thinks of instructing one of his bear-goons to drag Remo outside and beat him to death, but he doesn't. No, Crow is a pro. He decides to take lemons and make himself a big-ass pitcher of lemonade.

"New game," Crow announces as he walks over to the table, picking up the gun. He opens the cylinder and slides in two more bullets. "Three bullets total. One player. New odds."

The crowd perks up.

"Fuck," Remo says.

Crow motions to the woman and man seated at the table to take a seat on the couch. The woman tips the bottle at Remo as she slinks off, chugging some more. She could have at least left the bottle, Remo thinks. He did kinda save her life. Where's the fucking gratitude in the world?

Now it's Remo against three bullets.

"Clear the books, taking new bets," Crow calls out.

There's a new shot of energy to the room. A new buzz of excitement as money changes hands. Remo watches it all. Watching this new level of inhumanity in these people is leaving him numb. It was there before, sure, but at least then they had a share in the risk. They could catch a bullet in the skull just as easily as Remo. Now they are basically looking to profit off a forced suicide.

Are you entertained?

Crow shoves the revolver into Remo's hand. "If you're thinking about taking that piece, pointing it at me and squeezing the trigger until you put a bullet in the chamber, don't. My boys will cut you down before you get a single shot off."

He pats Remo on the shoulder as he turns and walks back over to his spot by the vault door. Nestled between his trusty bear-goons.

The sudden change in the house rules of the game has removed some of his scotch high, but make no mistake, Remo is still drunk. He starts to laugh uncontrollably. Shaking. A hard laugh that starts with a chuckle and snort but grows into an intense silence. His mouth and eyes wide open. The gun quivers back and forth in his hand. Tears roll down his face. Remo can't decide if this is truly funny or a full-blown mental meltdown. Crow and the crowd watch, not sure what to do with this. They look to one another. Remo pulls himself together, waves the gun around. Everyone ducks.

"Let's get this over with, okay people?" he says, standing up.

Remo puts the gun to his head.

In his mind he can see the bullet leave the chamber.

"This what we all want here tonight?"

He hopes Sean will understand his father someday.

Remo pulls the trigger.

Click.

He snorts a laugh, dropping the gun to his side, then quickly raises the gun back up stabbing himself in the temple with the barrel.

"Wait," yells Crow. "They have to place their bets." He motions for the Dapper Man to stop him.

The Dapper Man grabs Remo's hand, trying to pull the gun away. Remo fights him by yanking the gun back. They both have their hands locked around the gun as they sway side to side, moving in a circle.

Spit flies from the Dapper Man's mouth as he pulls at the gun with all he has. "Give me the damn gun."

"Go fuck yourself, slick."

"Slick?"

Blam.

The back of the Dapper Man's head explodes.

A collective gasp from the room. Wide-eyed stares all around.

Pin-drop silence.

Dapper Man's body slumps to the floor.

Remo shrugs.

The ceiling above the table cracks then crumbles down. Chunks of plaster drop at first. A muted pop sound echoes, then another. A large section of the ceiling the size of a piano comes crashing down, showering the floor with debris.

Remo wastes no time analyzing the situation. He rips the six-shooter from the Dapper Man's dead hand. Spinning around he turns the gun on Crow, squeezing the trigger.

He feels an unsatisfying *click.*

"Fuck me," Remo barks.

People scatter away from the couches like roaches when the lights come on. Hollis drops down onto the table, blasting his sawed-off as he lands. The rhythmic pumps burst, cutting up bear-goons left and right. Blood and meat pop and spread across the vault-like door as the bodies drop like oversized sacks of dirt. Crow dives clear, lead peppering the air his face occupied a split-second ago.

Remo runs at Crow with all he has. Releases a primal scream, putting his shoulder down. Crow pivots like a matador. Remo misses his mark, slamming face-first into the vault door, his cheek slip-sliding across the slick, fresh bear-goon blood.

Crow hauls ass toward the back.

Hollis blasts away at Crow as he races by, exploding couch cushions, tables and walls along the way. Crow grabs a guest by the suit jacket, pulling him along, using him as a human shield. The guest takes a shot in the chest. A red burst sprays the air as Crow releases his jacket, dumping the deadweight to the floor. Hollis pumps, blasts again. A bear-goon is blown back over the bar. Crow bolts out a door that was previously hidden by the darkness. A door-sized shaft of light cuts through the room, revealing gun smoke spiraling upward, along with the aftermath of sudden mayhem. Screams roar. Guests trample over other guests. Blood pools on the floor.

Remo gets to his feet, charging hard at the door after Crow. He pushes a guest to the floor on his way out, manages to put an elbow into the woman who stole his bottle, putting a little extra humph on it.

Hollis jumps down from the table. He has his Nike bag over his shoulder. Digging into the bag he pulls out his second sawed-off. "Remo."

As Remo turns Hollis tosses him the shotgun. Remo wants to lay into Hollis's ass about being late more than anything, but even Remo knows now is not the time. Hollis showed up. Remo is alive and that's what matters. Later, at a time of his choosing, Remo will tear him a fresh one.

Remo and Hollis burst out of Crow's place, spilling into the streets of New York. Remo fights to get his vision right after coming out of the dark room and stumbling into the blinding light of day. He bounces off a light post and a few not-so-understanding New Yorkers. His face is smeared with bear-goon blood, he's drunk as a motherfucker, carrying a sawed-off shotgun, but that doesn't mean a damn thing to Remo. He has one thing on his hammered mind, and that thing is killing Crow.

Hollis is running beside Remo, with Crow up ahead by a few car lengths. Remo raises his sawed-off one-handed while running at top speed down the busy street. There's a scream behind him. Hollis quickly reaches over, shoving the gun down. Not a great idea to fire a shotgun while burning ass down a busy city street. Many reasons. Too many to cover now.

Hollis and Remo push harder. Legs churn. Thighs burn. Lungs pumping acid. They're gaining on him.

There's a busy intersection up ahead.

They know they need to get him before he crosses. High odds of losing him in that mess.

Crow cuts and weaves between the throngs of people packed along the street. Remo and Hollis follow with relentless determination. Crow flies across the street. Remo hits the curb, about to jump across as Hollis grabs him by the collar, pulling him back. A massive city bus rips down the street, almost taking Remo's nose with it.

A split-second after the bus blazes past, Hollis and Remo take off as if a starter's pistol fired. Their heads whip around, looking for Crow. He could have gone in any direction. Panic starts to set in.

"Over there," Hollis says.

Crow has put some distance between them, but they can still see him cutting through the crowded streets up ahead.

They push harder.

Sirens wail behind them.

Hollis looks back. Cops are back there, coming fast.

"Running out of time," Hollis yells at Remo.

Remo doesn't care. He pumps his legs harder and harder. Crow is putting some distance between them. He can taste killing him. Remo's not a murderer, but he could really get into killing a piece of shit like Crow. Many people could.

Sirens get louder. Closer.

Crow races across another clogged street.

Remo and Hollis are on him, in pursuit like focused bloodhounds, but Crow is getting farther and farther away.

"Shit," Hollis spits.

Sirens wail a few blocks back.

Remo feels hope slip. They're going to lose him. After all this, he's going to get away with it.

Again.

Lester slams Crow hard to street.

Hollis and Remo can't believe what they're seeing. From out of nowhere, Lester wraps his tatted-up arms around Crow's ribs planting him to the concrete. A full-on, brutal NFL sack. Crow's head bounces off the sidewalk, leaving a blood spot. Lester pins Crow's arms down with his knees and begins beating him mercilessly with his prison-tested fists. Thick thumps of skin beating skin. Cracks. Crunches of skull. Blood spurts. A crowd builds up, surrounding them.

Hollis and Remo reach the crowd. Hollis pulls Lester off of what's left of Crow. Lester screams and spits like a wild dog having his bone taken away. This is the dark side of Lester. The side that deserved to go to prison. The side you don't want to be on the wrong end of. The side that cut off Dutch's head.

Lester catches his breath and notices the blood on Remo's face. Touching him, he says, "You okay?"

Sirens are even closer now.

"Fantastic," says Remo. "We gotta get gone."

The three partners-in-mayhem burn ass away from the scene. Lester leads them right, then left then down an alley. Lester's suitcase sits near the back of a restaurant. Lester grabs the handle as they race by, pulling it along behind him. The wheels skip, barely touching the ground.

Up ahead a white van screeches to a stop, closing off the exit to the alley.

They spin around. Another van cuts off the other end of the alley.

They're completely boxed in.

Hollis jams more shells into his shotgun.

Remo readies his with a pump.

Lester pulls a butcher knife from the suitcase with one hand and rips his Glock loose from his shoulder holster with the other.

They stand ready to face whatever special brand of asshole is about to come at them. United. Strong. A force that will not go quietly into that good or any other fucking night.

Fssst. A whisper-zip cuts through the air.

A tiny red dart lands in Hollis's neck with a thunk. His legs fold out from under him immediately, as if his legs gave up upon impact. Another dart sticks into Lester's neck. He pulls it out, tosses it aside, makes it two steps with his weapons raised. He screams, almost barks at them.

Fsst. Fsst. Double darts. Red blurs. One to the neck, one to the forehead.

Lester folds.

"Fuck this shit," Remo says, running full-throttle with his shotgun raised, screaming at the top of his lungs like an insane warrior from days past.

Fsst.

Remo's world goes black.

Insane warrior down.

33

Remo sits at the end of a long table made of polished stone.

He holds the guest of honor position in the middle of an exclusive private dining room. A little-known room located at the back of his favorite steak house. This room is reserved at a steep price, and is only for the special, elite folks of the city. You don't hear people talk about it and it is not offered to many.

Seated along both sides of the table are people Remo knows well.

To his right sits Hollis, Lester and the Mashburn brothers, whose names, in order of age and importance, are Dutch, Ferris and Chicken Wing. Dutch is the only one at the table without a head. It is, however, placed with care in front of Dutch, next to the butter plate but far enough away from the food that nobody gets too uncomfortable.

Nobody seems to care, not that kind of crowd, but you never know.

On the left side sit Detective Harris, what's left of Crow, the Dapper Man with a massive hole in his head, and big, bad CIA man Cormack.

At the far end of the table, directly across from Remo, is his son Sean, who is sitting in Remo's ex-wife Anna's lap.

All of the dinner guests look on, staring at Remo with glazed, emotionless eyes, but with smiles plastered wide as sunrises. It's as if they have all been heavily sedated, or possibly lobotomized, recently. They are all silently watching Remo eat. Not a word spoken or blink made as they watch on, soaking in the vision of Remo taking down the feast laid out in front of him. A feast fit for a king. A thick, perfect medium-rare filet is placed in front of him, along with the following: a loaded baked potato, a big-ass Caesar salad, thinly cut french fries, a plate of chicken fried rice the size of his face, a gorgeous apple pie, and a bottle of mother's milk—Johnnie Blue.

Remo swallows the last chunk of steak, wipes the red juice from his lips and washes it all away with a sip of Blue.

He looks to his guests. They still sit silently smiling his way. Remo sighs a massive sigh, shrugs his shoulders, then pushes away from the table.

As if on cue, Sean slips off his mother's lap and opens the door that provides an exit out the private room. Remo steps away from the table and pats his son's head as he passes through the door. The rest of the table stands and follows him out single file. Dutch brings his head.

Outside, the sun shines bright with clouds rolling across the bluest of skies. Remo takes his place in front of a red brick wall. He holds a glass of Johnnie Blue in his hand, taking a gulp as he turns around.

He's now facing a firing squad made up solely of his dinner guests.

They're all there, most with weapons pointed directly at him, but their smiles are long gone. They hold a variety of weapons. Mostly handguns, a shotgun or two, with the notable exceptions being Dutch, who has a WWII flamethrower, and Crow, who holds some Chinese throwing stars.

Anna and Sean are unarmed, but watch on.

Remo looks to Sean.

The little boy raises his thumb.

Remo exhales and smiles.

Sean turns his thumb down.

Remo nods and closes his eyes tight.

34

Remo's head feels like the inside of a used diaper.

Forcing his lids open, he only finds more darkness before him. Hints and rumors of light peak out via slits and slants but only at the margins of his vision. More like the light is along the bottom and sides of something. Actually, it's exactly like light is working its way through the cracks of something that's over Remo's head.

"Hello?" he says.

"Hello," says Hollis.

"Hello," says Lester.

"Hello, gentlemen," Cormack says.

Remo trembles like a bomb went off inside his chest. An anger-shake shudders from the tips of his toes to the top of his cloaked head. He tries to get whatever's covering his head off but realizes his arms are bound behind him. His feet are strapped to the chair he's sitting in. He's guessing zip ties. It's embarrassing to admit he knows what they feel like, but he can't help but admire the quality of the material. Nothing but the best for the CIA.

"Can you take this fucking thing off my head?" Remo asks.

There's a long pause.

"Are you shitting me? You need me to say please?"

Another long, drawn out pause.

Without warning, the bag is ripped away, blasting blinding light into his face. With one eye open and one closed tight, Remo looks around, seeing that Lester and Hollis are also both zip-tied to chairs next to him. As he adjusts to the light, he can see they are in a small room in what looks like a modest home. Walls painted in accessible beige. Shit pictures on the walls and blackout curtains pulled closed on the windows. No telling if it's night or day, let alone what day it is. There's a high-intensity light shining on each of them like they were being interviewed on a TV show. Remo, Lester and Hollis can safely assume they are no longer in NYC based on the fact there is no street noise. There's no noise at all. There is a dead silence all around. No cars. No talking. Not even a damn cricket.

Cormack leans in the doorway dressed in his standard navy blue CIA garb. The expression on his face can be described as expressionless. He's neither happy, sad, nor angry. He is simply there. Shifting slightly to the left, Cormack now leans on the other side of the door. He clucks his tongue, raises his eyebrows, then holds his hands out as if looking for questions from his captive audience.

"Where would you like to start?" Cormack asks.

Remo, Hollis and Lester look to one another. *This guy, this fucking guy.*

"How about kick it off with *what the fuck, man?*" Remo says. "Or, *where the fuck are we?* Perhaps, *what was the fucking deal with those fucking darts* and, last but not least, *what in the fuck are you doing with us tied up like a trio of fucking fuckheads?*"

"Your buddy bashed Crow's skull in on the streets of New York."

"So?" Lester asks.

"Yeah, so what? It's done," Hollis says.

"We did the thing, we took out Crow," Remo says.

Cormack clucks his tongue again. He looks to the ceiling for some form of divine strength. "How are we supposed to question Crow now? Huh? He's barely alive in a hospital room and if he does pull through he'll more than likely only be able to urinate blood and meow answers."

"Sounds like a *you* problem," Hollis says.

Lester nods.

"Look. If you wanted this handled a certain way, Cormack, perhaps you should have been a little more specific with your instructions," Remo says.

"Now I know," Cormack replies. "I'll make sure this next one is explained in much, much more detail."

Silent pause in the room. Looks between Remo and his partners in crime fire off. Confusion circling the three of them.

"Next one?" Remo asks.

"Yes," Cormack says. "Meaning the one after the one you just did. Specific enough?"

"Wasn't the deal, man," Remo says, gritting his teeth.

"Did you think there was a deal? That's adorable. There is not. The only deal is you do what I want until I say we are done or you're dead. Does that provide the clarity you boys seek?" Cormack turns, leaving the room.

Remo feels himself deflating.

As if his bones and muscles have been nullified by Cormack, and he could simply spill out onto the floor into a puddle of goo. Any hope Remo had of being a normal person or a somewhat normal father to Sean is slipping through his fingers.

Perhaps gone.

Forever.

Cormack stops after a few steps then turns back to the room. "Okay. That wasn't completely fair, what I just did there a second ago. Sorry. Let me reset, okay? This next one, the one you boys are going to do, it's a big one. To be honest it's the one I really brought you in to accomplish, Remo. Oh, big thanks by the way for bringing in Lester. I hoped you would, but it really brings this thing together."

Lester stares.

The old Lester would gut Cormack right here and now without a hint of hesitation. Actually, the new Lester is considering it.

"You clowns left a hell of a mess to clean up in New York, but don't worry, I'll take care of it. It'll give Detective Harris something to do," Cormack says, then snaps his fingers as if he remembered something. "I've got some cash and prepaid credit cards for you, along with the clothes and weapons you'll need. You know, a good faith measure to show we're all one team." Cormack extends a hand, showing someone in. "My new friend will fill you in. I gotta bounce."

Cormack leaves.

As he clears the doorway, in walks a woman dressed in jeans and a torn man's dress shirt that hangs on her two sizes too large. She wears no shoes, nails firing off neon green.

It's the woman from the hotel.

The one who brought back Dutch's head.

The one who attacked Lester and Hollis in the alley.

The one who keeps dropping off fast-food napkins.

Hollis's and Lester's eyes bug out.

"Get that woman the hell away from me, man," Hollis says, trying to squirm away while still in a chair that's bolted to the floor.

Lester just stares at her with eyes wide as pies.

Remo looks to them, then to her. "Wait. I know you?"

She smiles sweetly, twisting her hair around her finger. "I'm Cloris." She waves to Lester like a schoolgirl with a massive crush. "Cloris Mashburn."

Remo and Hollis whip their heads around to Lester.

Lester looks like he's just been kicked in the balls. Twice.

"Mashburn?" Remo asks.

Cloris giggles, twisting her hair tighter. "As in Ferris, Chicken Wing and poor Dutch. Ya know? The head I delivered back to you. Those Mashburns. I'm the sister. Nice to meet you all." She looks to Lester. "You want to tell them what else, Buttercup?"

Remo's eyes slip to Hollis. *Buttercup?*

Lester shakes his head violently, like a toddler who doesn't want to admit he spilled grape juice on the new carpet.

Remo and Hollis are all ears, jaws on the floor.

"Lester and me, we're sweeties. As in engaged," she says, showing off her ring. "We're a bona fide thing."

THE END

COMING SOON

Book three in the Remo Cobb series.

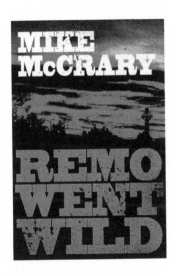

BOOKS BY MIKE MCCRARY

Remo Went Rogue
Remo Went Down

Genuinely Dangerous
Getting Ugly

ACKNOWLEDGEMENTS

I say the same thing with each book and I will continue saying it until it stops being true. You can't do a damn thing alone, so I'd like to thank the people who gave help and hope during this fun and self-loathing little writing life of mine.

The list of those people is insanely long and keeps growing by the day. The idea of leaving someone out and listening to them bitch later is a little more than I can take on right now. Not to mention, this Remo thing here is a series and I'm not sure I can hammer out a long list of thank you notes after each book. That's a lot, man. No matter how much you people may or may not deserve it. Another thing, do authors really want to thank all those people? Some of that has to be sucking up. I mean really, we're all grownups here. It's not show friends, it's show business, right?

So let's cut the proverbial shit.

Let's just say I am very thankful to all of you. Each one of you have helped me more than you can possibly know. I am truly grateful to those people who have helped me out and talked me off the ledge more times than I can count. This is me being honest, no bullshit here. Hopefully you know who you are.

Also, if you're reading this right now you deserve a big-ass thank you from me as well. Even if we've never met, you've been cool and kind enough to grab a copy of my book and give it a read and that, my dear friends, deserves the biggest ACKNOWLEDGEMENT of them all.

Thanks, good people.

ABOUT THE AUTHOR

I've been a waiter, a securities trader, dishwasher, bartender, investment analyst and an unpaid Hollywood intern. I've quit corporate America, come back, been fired, been promoted, been fired again. Currently, I write stories about questionable people who make questionable decisions.

Please stop by www.mikemccrary.com and sign up for my Reader's Group so you can get all the latest news on new books, special offers and various cool crap.